L.E. Usher has been a bookseller, an editor, and co-publisher of a magazine on women's literature. Born and educated in Australia, she currently lives in London.

Forthcoming from the same author

The Sudden Spoon

MISS

L.E. USHER

First published by Quartet Books in 1999
A member of the Namara Group
27 Goodge Street
London W1P 2LD

This edition published by Quartet Books in 2000

A catalogue record for this book is available from the British Library

ISBN 0 7043 8148 6

Printed and bound in Great Britain by Cox & Wyman, Reading, Berks

MISS

ONE

I dream of death. My death. By drowning. To dream of drowning is said to presage a life of sorrow, so I have read. I no longer remember which came first, the sorrow or the dream.

In this dream in which I am drowning I walk on sand. As I look towards the horizon, the sand which undulates endlessly laps at my feet to rise and tower over me in a wave whose spray sprinkles my face. I watch the wave tumble towards me and, as it strikes my face, I open my mouth and feel water fill my mouth and flow down my throat, its coldness seeping throughout the cavities of my chest, filling my lungs to such a capacity that the water that has poured in through my gaping mouth is forced upwards and gushes out of my nostrils.

All the while that this is happening my eyes remain open, fixed upon the endless wave tumbling into my mouth, until I realize that, in fact, I am dead. I have drowned. Then, I close my eyes.

I am a bookseller. I am also a book buyer and a book reader, and I have also on occasion been a book thief. The bookshop is mine, although it is not my name that swings on the sign that hangs outside the front door. That name, 'R. Hare', is the sole remnant of the eighteenth-century bookseller who once traded here. My bookshop is small: a long room replete with secondhand books. Three and a half days each week I open the bookshop to the public and sit behind my desk, buying and selling. On the other days I go down to the basement and wrap books to be sent in the post, layer upon layer, cushioning them against their journey to new homes around the world. My life is quite straightforward; in the evenings I go up the spiral staircase to my rooms above the shop and in the morning I come back down the spiral staircase, sometimes one flight, sometimes two, depending on which morning it is, clutching a pot of tea, at five minutes to ten, on the dot.

I enjoy living over the shop, it soothes me to know that these books are underneath me. For they *are* mine. I have paid for them and until someone else pays me for them they will remain mine. But above and beyond this financial exchange these books will always be mine for I have chosen them, taken them into my hands, raked my eye over their every detail, opened them and smelt their secret smell, and chosen them to sit on my bookshelves. I know these books, my books, inside and out. On a number of occasions I have refused a sale simply because I didn't like someone's face or their hands. I have taken my book back from them, apologetically stating that actually this particular book is not for sale. Understandably some of them argue — bemused tones turning to irritation and often belligerence. Most often they never return, which relieves me of the task of saying no a second time. Occasionally my rejected book buyers will walk past and stop and glare in the window at me or make a point of swinging their carrier bags from other bookshops as if to show me, to prove to me, that their custom is desirable elsewhere. That they are desirable as book buyers, as book owners. But some booksellers don't give a damn. So long as money crosses their palm, they would sell to anyone. I can't do that. I *will* not do that. How could I forgive myself if I sold a book to someone whom I disliked?

At this time of year when darkness hovers at four–thirty the bookshop is at its most beautiful. Actually, that is not quite true; the bookshop is always beautiful. On grey, gloomy days it seems murky and mysterious, while in sunshine the room shimmers with the light that bounces off book spines spinning linear rainbows. The thought alone makes me smile.

Today, as the darkness moves in to shroud corners, I sit behind my desk, and in the shop-window I can see my books reflected back at me, warmly glowing. If I stare hard enough I can make out my own reflection, smiling, but these days I find it difficult to see that far, and I am content to remain indecipherable. To my left is a pile of books that I am cataloguing, to my right the fire – real gas – flickers. At my back is a long window which takes up the entire wall and if I turn in my chair, resting my arm on the back, swinging my crossed legs to the side, I can see the ivy wavering at the back of the garden, climbing the brick wall that is as high as the house, and which blocks out the side street and the train station.

How many times have I been told by other booksellers, that my long window is unnecessary, such a waste of space, so many more books could be crammed into that space if it were turned into shelves. But I love that window – not a sentimental choice of word, for I *do* love it – allowing, as it does, the changing light streaming through it to flicker around my head and across my desk before moving around the room. I like to stand at the window looking down into the garden and watch my cats, while stretching my deskbound limbs in imitation of their movements.

Today has been quiet – Thursday afternoons often are. Sunday is my busiest day, in the afternoon when people go walking in the park. I was the first along here to open on a Sunday afternoon and now everyone does. For we are all booksellers of some description along this street. At the end of the day we occasionally retire to the pub on the corner, exaggerating our sales, being snide about our customers, subscribing in general to the bitch-and-moan society. For if there is one thing that is generally known about booksellers, it is that we are the most tireless whingers known to mankind. Besides, of course, that we are a queer bunch – queer, in the old-fashioned sense of the word – incapable of doing anything other than selling books.

But then, I would ask, what else is there that is really worth doing? Is there something apart, something above and beyond the buying and selling of books? Writing perhaps? I often think that all of us would like to be writers. But then, perhaps not. These days one doesn't even have to like books to be a bookseller, let alone think of writing them. How many times have I read in the newspapers that bookselling is big business, that books are a product, there to be marketed.

Product, my arse, I think, yet it is true that for many of my fellow booksellers, books have become merely objects. Meaningless beyond their price tag. A product to be marketed and sold. I often wonder what the world will be like in a couple of decades from now when booksellers such as myself have all disappeared.

For I love reading, love books, love words, and a life without books is beyond imagining. As I look around my bookshop and remember all the bookshops I have browsed through, all the libraries I have sat in, all the books I have read, I feel blessed. What else, what more could there possibly be?

Today there will be no gathering at the pub, at least not for me, not on Thursday's. In half an hour or so Edmund will be here, and if not, if he is unable to make it, he will telephone. It is our ritual, has been for years now, Edmund coming to tea on Thursday afternoons. Edmund Maskelyne. Doubtless you know the name. Few are unfamiliar with the name of Maskelyne. Even if you haven't read any of Edmund's five books. Five books. All on different subjects, all differing levels of mediocrity, all saluted by a grovelling press, indeed, as if an oracle had spoken. The Maskelyne oracle.

When I first met Edmund I had owned R. Hare for two years. I felt a little sorry for him. Poor Edmund, I thought, trying to write with the oppressive Maskelyne heritage suffocating him, one of the last to bear that literary name in a family whose weighty aura continues to permeate the writing fraternity. Those offshoots of the Maskelyne tree with their variety of surnames writing about poetry and cooking and gardening and opera and music and, let us not forget, each other's books. All accomplished with a grandiose vacuity. It took me some time, I'm ashamed to say, before I realized that being a Maskelyne was, in fact, the thing to be.

Edmund and I became friends, if an Englishman can be friends with a woman, that is. And so began our ritual of his coming to tea on Thursdays. Bringing sandwiches or biscuits, minding the shop for the ten minutes or so that it takes me to go upstairs and make a pot of tea. When we first met I also wrote. I still do, but I am not a talented writer and realize that if one is unremarkable it is necessary to have the connections that Edmund has, at least.

The result: *I* sell books, *Edmund* writes them. Each book no worse than the last, but progressively shorter, less and less wordy. Each on a different subject because he has no voice of his own. Or if he does, it is locked away somewhere inaccessible, deep within the wilderness recesses of his Maskelyne brain.

For some time I was fond of Edmund, it would be a lie to say otherwise. Initially I found his self-effacing wit charming, and the stories he told absorbing. Ultimately, however, I have come to see him as a coward. Despite his repeated verbal denigrations of his family, despite his verbal yearnings for independence, he has continued to manipulate the labyrinthine Maskelyne connections for the sake of his writing career.

Did I, perhaps, think that he might introduce me into the golden circle of the Maskelynes and that publishing doors would magically swing open allowing entry for my second-rate writings? But golden circles remain forever closed to outsiders, and all one is ever really allowed to do is tiptoe around their parameters, genuflecting occasionally.

Almost unthinkingly, I became contemptuous of Edmund's unmerited success until finally, with the publication of his most recent book, my resentment turned to rancour and paroxysms of rage. Of all the books to write: a biography of his grandmother, another bloody biography of Hermione Maskelyne to be added dutifully to the saturation of biographies already lined up on the bookshelf. Even more insulting: it was all lies. On the many Thursday afternoons that we passed here together, he has told me all about Hermione and his relationship with her. How she despised him and he feared her, feared her decimating sarcasm, both verbal and written. But does this feature in Edmund's biography? No. Instead the reader is treated to a little over a hundred pages of supposedly witty anecdotes. Amusing, perhaps, but only to sycophants. How abhorrent I found it. I wanted him to suffer. To suffer as I suffered as I read his facile drivel about Hermione. And so, I am plotting his death.

It is not a decision that I came to easily. For many months I have had all manner of elaborate fantasies concerning his death, the more gruesome the better. But eventually the frisson of pleasure, the excitement I felt at these fantasies, wore off, and they became repetitious and mechanical, as most fantasies do over a prolonged period of time, I suppose.

I cannot be precise as to when my thoughts turned to murder. In my memory the moment coincides with the purchase I made of a private library solely comprising a collection of books about women and crime. I went to view the library out of curiosity, not presuming that I would purchase, expecting to find modern pulp with garish covers. Which I did, alongside salacious treatments of lurid lives, raw unhappiness and palpable fear. Facile discourses on complex women. But amongst these I discovered much else besides: execution ballads and gallows broadsides, prison statements, court transcripts, biographies and autobiographies, some from as long ago as the early sixteenth century. Also rare leather-bound editions containing learned, as well as not-so-learned treatises on the criminal psyche. Novels. Poetry. Plays. All on women. Women criminals. Criminal women.

I was taken aback. Some of the women I had heard of, but in many instances I had regarded their tales as apocryphal. Little more than literary invention. As I looked I noticed that all the women included in this collection had displayed premeditation in the criminal acts they had committed. These were women whose crimes had been carefully plotted. Literate women, educated to some degree, who had each achieved notoriety within their own lifetime. These were not lives for which there were only fragmentary remains. And adding evocatively to the words relating to some individuals were painted and drawn images, helping to bring them to eloquent life.

The walls of that unexceptional terraced house where the collection came from were lined with overflowing bookshelves, organized chronologically, alphabeticized according to the type of criminal or crime committed: assassin, fratricide, homicide, infanticide, mariticide, matricide, parricide, patricide, poisoner, serial killer, sororicide, uxoricide. Women who had wielded the offending weapon, who had prepared the poison; women who had cannily used intermediaries such as a lover to commit the murderous act that they themselves had plotted. Even at a glance, I knew that the activities of these women oozed duplicity and ruthless opportunism, so that I was drawn into their crimes. They seemed intricate and labyrinthine, infinitely interesting. I was already riveted as I began to snoop through that tidy collection of untidy deeds.

We booksellers had been block-booked that day, each given an hour to browse alone. Before my hour was complete I knew that I wanted this collection. I was willing to pay more than was required to pack these books in cartons and take them back to R. Harè, there to slowly catalogue them and place them upon my bookshelves in reach of a customer's inquisitive hand. I scribbled my offer on the reverse side of my card and promised to confirm it in writing. I knew that the books were mine, no one else would be idiotic enough to offer such a high price. It took three days of packing and piling the cartons into the station-wagon to complete the move. The boxes − all fifty-six of them − were stacked throughout my rooms in the basement, with one placed underneath my desk which I would plan to catalogue. A box per week is the task I have set myself. I have another forty boxes left to do.

As I catalogued, I read. Uncovering extraordinary lives, many forgotten. In time I began to ask myself the question why, if women of such audacious criminal deeds had existed for centuries, did we find contemporary women murderers such a shocking anomaly? Without doubt, there were − there are − fewer female criminals than male, but here was proof that they were as capable of violence as their male counterparts. Where, I wondered, had the idea come from that contemporary women are growing more and more violent, that violent women are a post-modern phenomenon? With the blame resting on the combined result of television, lack of parental control, collapse of moral order, feminism? Survey after survey apparently confirm the facts. According to the books that I held in my hands there appeared to me to be a strong historical precedent for the current crop of women who killed.

Why, I asked myself, was not some psychologist or scholar or feminist historian retrieving this plethora of texts from the archives to state that history reveals a multitude of terrible deviations from what is considered the female norm?

We had been for lunch together, Edmund and I, with two of his friends, and the conversation had turned to a notorious female murderer and her potential release from prison. After too much alcohol, the conversation had degenerated into an argument, albeit a polite one, with myself on the side of the demoness from hell. If after thirty years in prison she has not been punished for her crime and so cannot be released, I argued, then surely capital punishment ought to be reintroduced. If she wasn't showing remorse or an awareness of her actions and remained a danger to society then obviously she should remain in prison. But she was remorseful, no longer a danger to society. If she could not be set free, if she was to remain guilty in perpetuity with no possibility of rehabilitation, then she and other murderers like her should be executed. If their acts were considered to be so inhuman that the only way for society to deal with the perpetrators was to lock them up until they died, then why should they not be executed and save the taxpayer a great deal of money?

I was playing devil's advocate of course, although I am not without sympathy for the belief in an eye for an eye and was, unsurprisingly, shouted down by my offended companions. The death penalty was barbaric. This woman deserved to stay in prison, did not deserve a normal life. I was asked, would the families of those she murdered ever have a normal life? It depended on what was considered a normal life, I responded. Imagine, I said, living with the knowledge that one's own self had participated in such horrific deeds, imagine acknowledging that terrible part of one's self and integrating it into the psyche, to live with the knowledge that this part was also there inside one, was part of the person one confronted in the mirror every morning. To live with the deed as only this woman could, the minute details solely within her own memory, taunting her, haunting her.

Ultimately we agreed to disagree and went our separate ways. I thought no more of our conversation, so many inebriated arguments had we had over the years, too many to remember. The following Thursday Edmund arrived as usual. The shop was quiet, we sat to play chess. Hardly had we begun than he attacked me, verbally, that is. Called me all manner of imbecile for my opinions on that vile monstrous woman. Denounced me as a fool. Ignorant. Ignorant. Ignorant.

As this monotonous litany went on and on, I imagined taking up the paperknife that rested near my left hand, saw myself thrusting it into his neck. Stabbing. Over and over. I imagined the blood, spurting onto the books, onto the floor. Imagined being left with a lifeless body that I didn't know what to do with. Imagined someone walking in to buy a book and seeing puddles of blood. Imagined that then I would have to kill them too so they couldn't call the police. Or perhaps, before I could kill them they would scream and run. And the police would come and I would be taken away and there would be no one to run the bookshop. And it would be sold and all my books would be dispersed, to God knows where.

No. But my hand trembled in anticipation of knifing and slicing and gouging skin. Edmund and I continued to play chess and when the game ended with his checkmate, we shook hands and parted, knowing that we would meet again the following Thursday. As I packed away the chessboard and answered the phone and dealt with customers, my mind churned. I would, I decided, murder Edmund. Slowly. Painfully. Quietly cause his death. Irritate his insides with poison so that he would, in fact, yearn for death, indeed, might even kill himself. Would that not be the ultimate murder, to cause someone so much pain that life became unbearable and they finished it themselves?

v

I have been reading books, searching for an accessible poison, something simple, something natural. So natural that it could be said to be an accidental death. I have found so many potential poisons that it makes me laugh, not out loud or uproariously, more of a contented snort, an expelling of air through my nostrils, much in the way a horse snorts before tossing its head and striding away to the other side of the paddock.

Today was the first day. Edmund has gone. Been and gone. Has drunk my carefully prepared poison. Somehow he always contrives to arrive when the shop is empty. He stops and looks at the books I have placed in the window and I, becoming aware of a shape blocking the glow from the street lights, look toward the window. Simultaneously, we both nod and smile. Once in, the door closed, we shake hands. It is always the same. I go upstairs – behind the beaded curtain, Edmund calls it – and for the ten minutes or so that it takes to make tea, he looks after the shop.

Today I am extra careful; I have prepared things this morning, puréeing the rhubarb leaves I have steamed, turning them into a watery snot-coloured mulch which I water down and add to Edmund's tea. I prepare the same tea for myself, we shall share a pot of poison. I can not have him becoming suspicious by my suddenly changing a routine we have shared for so many years.

Having made my list of poisons according to what is in season, it took only a single trip to the supermarket to find sticks of rhubarb. I delicately sorted through the red-pink stems, selecting only those with the leaves still attached. Just a few leaves. After all, I don't want to kill him on my first attempt, just make him sick.

I pour his tea and watch him take a sip after he has added his usual two sugars. I place my cup to the side and watch the steam rise and disappear. He flares his nostrils and asks me what on earth I've given him, sucking his tongue against the roof of his mouth at its bitterness. Rhubarb and green apple, I tell him. Granny Smith, which is why it is bitter. We always drink fruit tea together, another of our rituals. Edmund's constitution can tolerate neither caffeine nor tannin, so it has always been a challenge to find different fruit teas to drink.

Lucky really. For me that is, not for Edmund. He adds more sugar, finishes his cup and pours another. I watch him and can almost feel the warm liquid travelling down his throat, down to his stomach, where it shall start to work on his system, giving him gut-ache, then cramp-like pains, and the urge to vacate his bowels, repeatedly. Even though there is nothing left to come out.

Our conversation is desultory. Today, he stays only an hour. There are our usual snide comments about the people that we know, someone's potential impotency, someone's disagreeable children, someone's foot infection. Edmund is a typical Englishman, terribly pleasant to your face but as soon as your back is turned he loses no time in sticking in the knife. I'm sure he ridicules me as well when he is speaking with other people. Why should he not? Why should I be the exception to the rule?

Shortly following Edmund's departure, his friend, Eliza, arrives. It is fifteen minutes or so before I close the shop, but she is Edmund's friend so I remain open just for her. I recall meeting her for the first time, how haughty she had been, taking my hand in her icy grip then aloofly disengaging it. I was, and remain, an admirer of her work, purchasing copies of her books which she signs for me in her ornate hand: Eliza Looker. Her writing and photographs, obsessed as they are with Roman Catholic rituals, are not understood in England, her following is on the Continent. Edmund has known her most of his life. His father had been her mother's lover before either of their marriages. They all knew each other, these people, were linked in an unnaturally inbred English way. Once I had asked him if he and Eliza had been lovers, but he said not, rather that she was more like the sister he had always wished he had.

Edmund had thought that she and I might be friends, but for some reason on that first introduction, we had sniffed around each other like cats, measuring the sharpness of each other's claws, before slinking away from each other, tails high in the air. Edmund had been surprised at the animosity I displayed, telling me to flatter her next time, for she was susceptible to flattery. Then after he had thought about it some more he changed his mind, saying that actually we were not dissimilar, but then refused to elaborate how. I, myself, could not see it.

We talk occasionally when she visits the bookshop, *she* talks I should say. Eliza is, I believe, slightly mad, I never disagree with her, never. Just let her talk until she runs out of words, which does not take long. As she pays for the books that she wishes to take, the long sleeve of the black shirt she wears will slide up to reveal burn like scars meandering around her wrist and along her arm. Sometimes when she is talking, engrossed in a story, her fingers will trace her scars, in a delicate playful way. On these days, I will admit, I feel relieved when she finally leaves, clutching her carrier bag full of books and I am able to lock the door behind her.

I was born on December 27th, 1964, in outback New South Wales. My mother, Mary Miss, and my father Mackie McCloskey, were not married, and never did marry although they were together for twenty-seven years. I was born at three in the afternoon, in the midst of a dust storm, opening my eyes to a gritty dun-coloured light. Downstairs Mackie played cards and drank whisky, in the saloon of the pub in which we were staying. Since my parents' first meeting they had temporarily stayed in many such places and my arrival did not hamper their wanderings during the next seven years.

I was christened Mary Miss McCloskey by a bush priest with a cup of brownish water scooped from the Darling River. So as not to cause confusion, I was always called Miss. Never Mary, for that was my mother's name. Only in retrospect do I wonder if my mother found it curious to call me by her own surname, by the name of the father of whom she never spoke.

Mary and Mackie's meeting could never have been foreseen. Involved in a war for which he had lied about his age to enter, he had been sent from Sydney to Egypt, where he had been injured and subsequently evacuated to England, there recuperating in the hospital in which Mary worked. Although he had lost an eye, and was later fitted with a glass one, he said that it only took one eye to tell that Mary was a bonza sheila. It was many years after his death before Mary told me that his injury had not been a war wound, but had been incurred when drunken revelry had turned nasty in a fight, she presumed, over a woman.

Mary had felt sorry for Mackie, released from hospital, discharged with nowhere to go, his home on the other side of the world, and so she smuggled him into the nurses' residence where she lived. She was soon discharged herself, unceremoniously turfed out, accused of being a whore, a disgrace to her uniform. Her parents, telephoned to come and remove their daughter, informed Mary that the choice was hers: she could either come home with them and marry a suitable local boy or be locked away, for no decent girl would behave as she had done unless she was insane.

Her response was to run away, with Mackie. The seventeen-year-old Australian soldier, whose army no longer required his services, and the nineteen-year-old nurse ran off together, continually moving, living a peripatetic existence for most of the following decade. Initially in England for the final few months of the war, they then moved on to Europe joining the floods of displaced people who wandered the length and breadth of the Continent. They did any job they could find to earn a living. Anything. Everything. Picking olives in Spain, grapes in France, following the sun. Occasionally they lied about their marital status and would get jobs as live-in staff, Mackie as a gardener, Mary as a maid. But these jobs never lasted long due to Mackie's trigger-temper; someone would only have to look at him, in a way that he would describe as askance, and in he would storm, fists flailing.

When I was older and Mary spoke about those times she made them sound like a perpetual adventure, a never-ending summer. Despite being poor, they had become such adept thieves that they never went hungry. But after a decade of moving around Europe and North Africa, Mackie became homesick, pining for the wide Australian spaces, so they both applied for jobs on a ship that would get them to the other side of the world.

Landing at Sydney, Mackie cried. Mary always seemed embarrassed when relating this part of the story, her gaze would go inward as she recalled Mackie's one good eye weeping, his face contorted like a lost child.

They immediately set out for the bush, wasting no time in searching out a family Mackie did not wish to see. He had missed the enormous empty beauty, not the family he had left behind. As far as he was concerned, Mary was his family. He revelled in the red earth baking in the sun which in drought would crack so wide apart that he could slide his hand, up to the wrist, inside the fissure. He awoke to the shriek of the galahs in the early morning chill and as the day grew hotter would sit with his back against the bark of a ghost gum tree and breath in the pungent smell of trees and earth in baking heat as he waited for his fishing line to quiver signalling supper was on the way. It was the happiest she had ever seen him, Mary said.

It was to be another decade before I was born, but even then they still kept moving, up and down the Darling River, following one of its tributaries up into Queensland, travelling down the Castlereagh River, further down the Macquarie to fruit fields, and along the Lachlan into cotton country, always following the meanderings of some river. When it was hot we slept under the stars, and when it was cold or raining we would sleep in the van, Mary and Mackie in the back, while I would be on the front seat with my head safely tucked under the steering wheel.

Years passed in a flash – in a blur, rushing by the van window. I grew, little Miss, becoming bigger. Playing around the fruit trees while my parents picked whatever was in season, learning very early on the small tasks that pleased them. Learning to thieve, in and out in a flash, while Mary or Mackie, or Mary and Mackie, kept the owner of the store occupied. At night I was allowed to play with Mackie's glass eye and would watch in fascination as the skin surrounding the ball collapsed inwards filling the empty hole. Patiently he taught me how to replace the glass so as not to hurt the scar tissue that surrounded the socket. As my childhood chatter grew with my height I also learnt the art of being still, especially when Mackie would point his glass eye eerily in my direction while closing his good one and mutter that Miss could talk a glass eye to sleep.

I was seven and had never been to school; although they had taught me to read and write I was not as proficient as I should have been. I never played with other children – my parents kept their distance from the other travellers, whom Mackie sneeringly called gypsies and tinkers. I lived in a fantasy world of colouring-in books and fairy stories, my toys the stones and twigs and leaves that I found wherever we stopped. Would I have disdained my parents' nomadic lifestyle as I grew older? Would I have resented them? Taken up with some boy as many of the traveller girls did in an attempt to get away from their parents? Only to find themselves mothers at fourteen, trapped in a life similar to their parents'. Is this what would have been my fate but for Mackie's death?

It didn't happen though and what is the point of endlessly

surmising? Fantasizing a life lived in and out of the back of a van, squatting behind trees to pee, looking to check that I'm not squatting over a bull ants' nest, that there are no snakes, no lizards, no crawlies of any type waiting to make their way onto my backside, or even worse inside my knickers.

Mackie's death came suddenly. We had camped off a dusty track, in the bend of a river, pulled the van over and set up half a mile from the orchards where they were picking apples. One evening Mackie didn't return, nor the next, nor the next. He had walked into the town three miles away and not returned. Mary was calm, and went to work in the orchard over the days that followed. Incredible as it later seemed she didn't drive the van into town in search of him. Telling me later, many years later, that she had known something awful had happened, but didn't want to pursue it, didn't want to go in search of it. She preferred to wait for it to make its way to her, as she knew it would.

It took a week. Three policemen drove up, with a photograph of Mackie, who had been found dead near the side of the road where he had slipped in a drunken stupor and struck his head on a rock. Mary drove the van into town, with me at her side, and went to the morgue to claim his body. She was asked to sign the papers at the morgue, no inquest was required, it was an accidental death. The local coppers weren't bothered about looking into the event too deeply. As far as they were concerned one of the travellers had become leery in the pub, been asked to leave, had declined, had been escorted from the pub and last been seen, according to pub eye-witnesses, walking down the road.

It was the small things that I would remember from that day. Sitting in the van in the sweltering heat with the vinyl seat sticking to my legs and sweat running down my armpits and flies sticking to my eyes, waiting while Mary was in the morgue, identifying Mackie. I remembered a copper buying me an orange ice from which I proceeded to suck all the colour and then rubbing the ice on my forehead and the back of my neck to cool myself down. I remembered Mary looking pale as she got back into the van and sat behind the steering wheel. I remember thinking that the heat must be too much for her, how she often went pale and wobbly in the heat — Mary's thin English blood, Mackie always said. How I had knelt on the seat and blew my orange-ice breath on Mary's temple where the sweat had soaked her hair, in an attempt to cool her down. I can still feel the shock as Mary swung her head away and landed me a resounding slap across the face that made my head throb. I remember feeling confused because in the past Mary had always loved it when I blew on her temple, would close her eyes, with a little smile curling the corners of her mouth. But now, suddenly, she didn't.

I didn't grieve for Mackie, nor miss him when he left our life. By the age of seven I had already realized that life was comprised of a series of people whom I would never see again. Mackie had merely joined that list. We left him there, Mary and I, then moved on. So I suppose that when I think of Mackie, I think of him still there, by the van down the dirt-track, frozen in time, standing, hands on hips, curious as to where Mary and I have got to. An image like a photograph so clear and strong is it in my mind.

The town cemetery refused to take Mackie so we buried him in a square plot on the outskirts of town, a cemetery that was literally a fenced-in piece of scrubland. Not even the tiny church remained in one piece and it was now derelict, a ghost church. This cemetery was for those whom the town declined to claim as one of their own. Murderers, suicides, lunatics, itinerants, hobos, alcoholics, many with no home, and long-forgotten names. We left Mackie there. Left him to moulder away in a plot full of forgotten people, and never went back. In the intervening years the dirt and stones will have sunk, and sometimes I wonder if there is any sign at all that a grave is there. I wonder whether the town has spread and houses have been built on the site and if perhaps it is now a garden where children play on a swing, and a father mows the lawn.

If I look I can still see it, as if I am standing there. Holding my mother's hand, I can feel the sun beating down on my head through the sun hat that I have been forced to wear, can feel the burrs and thistles pricking my feet and ankles. I can smell the eucalyptus trees and hear the wood creaking in some limb of the ghost church as I fight off the boredom that a child knows when involved in adult activities that it doesn't understand. I can still turn my head and gaze off into the distance and see the weeping willows draped along the riverbank and feel the hope that when this is over Mary and I will go for a swim and be lucky enough to find a pool that is free of leeches.

I don't think of Mackie at all. Not for a moment.

TWO

I awake, heart thudding. I push myself up in bed so as not to feel the pounding of my heart reverberating against the mattress. It is five in the morning and still dark, there seem to be few stars to glimpse through the clouds being forced across the sky. I lean my head against the window and look down into the garden. In the half-light I see my honeysuckle swaying in the wind and it makes me uneasy. My eyes seek out the dark corners of the garden and I dwell on what perhaps hides down there, unseen, before moving up to the basement door and trying the handle, gently at first, then pushing harder, attempting entry with each repeated push. Then, finding no access there, climbing the trellis, up to the first floor, peering in through the window whose length reveals shelves upon shelves of books. Then climbing again, trying the kitchen window to see if it will open. Did I lock it? I don't remember. I always lock it, don't I? But I don't remember. I'll have to go down and check. Down the stairs in the dark, on tiptoe so it can't hear me, peeking over the railing to see if I can see it at the window, its eyes looking up to catch mine, smiling as the window lifts.

Stop it. Stop it, for Christ's sake. I switch the light on, then switch it off. I have never liked the way the light turns the window into a black hole, a mere pane of glass between myself and the void. At least whatever is out there will have seen the light go on then off quickly, will know not to try the door or the window for I am awake and alert to every faint creak of my house as a warning of danger.

Of course I know that there is nothing out there. That I am unnecessarily frightening myself. How many times during my life have I woken, heart pounding, and thought that my dressing gown hooked on the end of the bed was crouched there waiting to pounce, known that if I bent to look under the bed I would meet a pair of eyes staring into mine. Known, known, known, in the depths of my being that there is something waiting for me to look its way. Some thing. Alive. Breathing.

Perhaps I want to be scared.

What would I do if the police came tomorrow and said Miss McCloskey, we believe that you gave Edmund Maskelyne rhubarb leaves, which are poisonous and that you did it knowingly. What would I say? Would I casually shrug and respond that I had actually drunk the tea as well, so how could it have been poisonous? Would they say so you won't mind if we look through your notebooks and journals? I would have to say of course not, shall I get them for you, hoping to hide the one that has all the notes about poisons that I jotted down in the library. Perhaps they would catch me hiding it and this notebook is all the evidence they would need to prove that I have plotted to poison Edmund. At least I wouldn't be hanged. The English don't hang their murderers any more.

Perhaps I *should* be scared.

Perhaps I should be careful and do something with my notebook of poisons, so that when Edmund is dead there will be no evidence that could be used against me. Just in case.

I start as one of the cats leaps onto the bed and pads towards me purring. Sure enough the other two follow quite quickly. I slide under the covers and they settle themselves in prearranged positions, with no squabbling. Their warmth soothes me, their solid masses curving into and around my body reassure me.

The wind drives sleet into my face as I walk along with hands thrust deep into my pockets, hands that although gloved ache from the cold and are locked at the joints. I push open the door and my face stings with the sudden respite from the sleet as I move into the portal and look through the glass of a second door into the church where a service is taking place.

A service? At eleven on a Monday morning? For God's sake. I can't go in, not while there is a service on because I'm sure that is the corner where she is interred, right there where, through the glass, I can see the shadows of a group of people seated. I lean my forehead against the glass, eyeballs aching from the cold. Fuck you, Mary, I whisper. Still hiding after all these years.

Leaving the church I look down the path to the right, past the headstones, past the tree with red berries, past the alms-houses, and try to conjure her walking along the path towards me, towards the church, to attend a service in the place where she had been baptized and where she would be buried thirty-three years later, hanged as a murderer. It is a path she would have taken many times but I can't see her, can't quite get a grasp on her, not even a glimpse.

There is nothing in Henley-on-Thames to say that she lived here. No little blue plaque claiming Mary Blandy, murderess, as resident. There is nothing, no thing at all to mark her presence, although she is buried in the church beside the father whom she poisoned. I'll wait, I turn back to the church and whisper. I'll wait for you, Mary. I want to stand over you and imagine you turning in your grave, coyly burying your lipless grin into the disintegrating fabric of a pillow, knowing that I've come in homage.

I retire to the pub and determine to give them an hour to do whatever they are up to in the church, and as I ease back in my seat with a whisky and green ginger wine a fleeting, fantastical thought occurs to me that perhaps I have witnessed ghost shadows organized by Mary to keep me away, to keep me at bay. Perhaps she wishes to elude me, not wanting to be known as a murderess. As I feel the heat of the whisky seep through my chest to land in my gut, I shake my head to clear it of such ridiculous thoughts. I am getting carried away. During the past week I have read how many books about her? Thirty? No wonder I'm feeling a bit queer in the head.

Mary Blandy and Elizabeth Jeffries: who riveted England in 1752. Mary who murdered her father, of this I am in little doubt despite her protestations of innocence. And Elizabeth who murdered her uncle, a pathetic greedy crime by a pathetic greedy girl. Imprisoned at the same time they had apparently corresponded. Mary writing to Elizabeth urging her to confess her crime. The arrogance of it, of Mary's patronizing social superiority in writing to the younger girl advising her to confess to save her soul, when she should have been contemplating her own soul. And Elizabeth had confessed. The day after being found guilty she had signed her confession. It is there in the Public Records Office, the signed original. But the letters have gone, all that remains of them are references in other texts, repeated quotations.

I get myself another whisky and green ginger, a double this time. I am beginning to thaw out, and remove my gloves and coat. Forty-five minutes to go. I stretch out my legs and close my eyes. I mustn't fall asleep. Mary, the well-bred daughter of the town clerk, living in genteel

Henley, making the trip to Bath in search of a husband, mingling with the local gentry. Elizabeth, the niece of a butcher retired to Walthamstow, sharing her uncle's bed, mistress of his house. How different would Henley and Walthamstow have been in the 1740s? Both rural villages, both on rivers, the Thames and the Lea. Fairly similar one would imagine. Mary. Elizabeth. The Fair Parricides.

On the evening prior to her hanging Elizabeth asked for her coffin to be brought to her cell in prison. She wanted to try it for size, and doing so finds, to her consternation, that it is too large for her around the shoulders. But because she is to leave for her execution at five the following morning it is too late for the fault to be remedied. So she folds inside the coffin the clothes that she will wear to her execution – a plain cap with a ribbon to tie it, a calico shift, and a pair of white stockings – then replaces the lid and lies upon the coffin for most of the long night.

Does she sleep well, I wonder? Or do the tips of her shoulder blades press painfully into the wooden lid so that she has instead to lie on her side, one hand palm up under her face, knuckles against the wood, the other hand tucked in close to her chest resting near her breasts. Is she calm, or fearful, or merely pleased that she is lying on top of the finest coffin imaginable – for she had chosen the best that money could buy – black, with a black plate and handles, lined and quilted with white satin. Paid for with the money she has received from the will of the uncle she murdered.

Mary, for her part, has made no provision for herself after her execution presuming, perhaps, that she will be given a last-minute reprieve. Following the hanging, her body suffers the indignity of being flung over the shoulder of one of the Sheriff's men and is carried through the crowd gathered in Oxford to witness her execution. Instead of being laid in some private place while a coffin is found and a hearse organized to remove her remains, her body is carelessly deposited on a table in the house of the Sheriff's man until she is finally brought the distance from Oxford to Henley and hastily buried in St Mary the Virgin. Interred with her parents.

I glance at my watch. The alcohol has warmed me, my cheeks burn, I am flushed. Fifteen minutes to go. Time for one more drink. I lift myself from the seat, a fluid easeful action. Warmth. Whisky. As I ask for another double, I am sure the barman wonders whether I have a drink problem. I don't look the type – young, female, polite, clean, tidy. I know I don't look the type – but who can tell these days.

They had prepared for their deaths in entirely different ways. Or should I say, one of them had prepared, the other had not. A drawing of Elizabeth from the time of her imprisonment in Chelmsford shows her to be an ordinary young woman of twenty-six years, round-cheeked, with a placid gaze. She is, however, not too bright and this is evident in the crime, which is a thoroughly bungled job. An onlooker at the trial describes her as having 'no malevolence in her countenance, nor indeed much sensibility. . . instead a kind of stupid inattention sat on her features'. But not an ignorant country girl by any means. Educated, able to read and write, and with imagination enough to plot a murder. But unfortunately only half-heartedly, in the belief that the details would somehow sort themselves out.

On the surface it seems a standard case. A young woman murders her uncle with the assistance of her lover because she is being threatened with exclusion from her uncle's will. Underneath the situation is more complex, for Elizabeth has been involved in an incestuous relationship with her uncle for nearly a decade. Five years prior to his murder her uncle, Joseph Jeffries, writes his will bequeathing all he owns to Elizabeth, naming her his sole executrix, a fact of which she is aware at the time. It seems, though, that it was not only greed that motivated her, for in her confession she states that she had been contemplating Joseph's murder for only a year prior to the act. The event which triggers the plotting, she declares, is his neglect of her after she had discovered him in bed with one of the household maids.

So, Elizabeth envisages not only her place in Joseph's affections being usurped but her inheritance disappearing as well. She is not his wife and could never be. She has no legal claims on him whatsoever. Yet she is dependent upon him financially as well as emotionally. Trapped and powerless. Thoughts churn in her mind, spiralling out of control and backing her into a dark corner. The only glimmer of light is the thought of financial independence, possible only upon the death of Joseph.

With her lover, named Swan, who has to be enticed into assisting with the promise of financial reward, Elizabeth begins to plot the murder. She plans to pass it off as one committed by a gang of robbers, but fails to pay enough attention to the finer points of her plan.

It takes the court only an hour to find Elizabeth and Swan guilty. It is difficult to say what is held against them more: Joseph's slow death or Elizabeth's extravagant behaviour while still a suspect and later after her arrest. For it took Joseph twenty-four hours to die. Incompetently shot by Swan, and incapable of speech, he slowly bled to death. During these twenty-four hours

Elizabeth irretrievably alienates her uncle's gathered friends by rifling through the contents of a box which contains his will, evidently unable to wait for his death before confirming that she is still his heiress.

As I put down my glass, I think of her and am perplexed. Can she, can they, really have been so stupid? The pistol that had been used was one of Joseph's own and Swan had been seen in the kitchen loading it earlier in the evening. The murder was too poorly planned to be merely a coldly calculated deed. Elizabeth's greed had got the better of her, clouding her judgement.

On the morning of her execution she is not indifferent to what awaits her. She dresses, fingers fumbling in the cold March air, looking at the coffin in which her dead body will soon lie, to have the horror of her actions come sweeping over her. For when they come to place the handcuffs on her wrists, she swoons and has to be carried from her cell to the waiting cart. During the long journey from Chelmsford to Epping Forest, where the gibbets wait, she falls into a fit which lasts half an hour – the convulsions so strong that although she is tied to the cart it takes three persons to hold her steady. And her former lover tied alongside her; what does he think of Elizabeth in her pretty calico dress, knowing that she will receive a Christian burial in her fancy coffin, but that after he is cut down from the gibbet he will be hung in chains for the crows and rooks to pick clean?

iii

Whisky-warmed through and through, I stride down the road to the church and, damn me, if it isn't still occupied, if I cannot still see through the glass, shadows seated.

I give up. I give up, Mary. Today I won't stand over your head and whisper through the flagstones that I know that you are guilty. Not today. Rest in peace.

Back at the car I realize that I am not in a fit state to drive. I need tea and a sandwich. I manage to seek out a cappuccino and a baguette meagrely filled with lettuce and tomato. As crumbs sprinkle my lap and the car seat with each mouthful that I take, I glare through the window at the Thames, at the groups of tourists watching the river greyly glide by, staring as if they had never seen a river before. I look at them in their multicoloured parkas, faces hidden under hoods, buffeted by wind and rain, feet getting soaked, and suddenly I want to be at home. I desperately want to close my eyes then open them and be in my room, ensconced on the sofa with the cats, not here in Henley feeling my whisky-induced well-being wearing off leaving me cold and damp and more than a little irritable. Today I can't be arsed to go on to Oxford to search out the spot where Mary was hanged, nor the gaol, nor the building in which she was tried. In my mind's eye, I can see it all already. I don't need to be there, surrounded by bedraggled parka-clad tourists. As I drive past the church I wave, tug my forelock so to speak, and the solid church door swings open. For a second there is nothing, then they that were shadows spill out onto the path.

iv

I clench my jaw and immediately force myself to relax. Edmund tells me that last week after his visit, slightly trepidatious about the bitterness of the tea I had given him and concerned for his sensitive tum, he had drunk a

35

pint of milk. He smiles sheepishly. I don't smile at all. Milk, natural antidote to rhubarb poisoning. I raise my left eyebrow and in the most casually exasperated voice I can manage I say you and your tiresome gut.

Actually, I am surprised to see him, given the weather. It has blown a gale all day and on the preceding evening the winds had caused fatal accidents. Today the winds have abated only a little but the rain has been perpetual, bucketing down, slashing this way and that. Yet here is Edmund, out in this weather to come to tea; yes, the type of moron to come out and then get struck by a piece of flying debris and have his skull cracked open.

What is it about the English? Today they have been out in droves, braving the elements to buy books. Are their lives so banal that it takes an excursion in gale force winds to make them feel alive, to give them a point of conversation? For that has been the sole topic today – the weather. The wind, the rain. With the English it is always the weather, but today there is an element of thrilled excitement in the tones of the wind-blown dripping specimens who have arrived in the shop. It is even there in Edmund's voice, as he continues to glance out of the windows – back and front – to make sure that the elements are still there, wind and rain united in hysteria.

I raise my eyebrow once more and inform him that I won't do rhubarb and green apple again if it's only going to make him anxious, adding, as he tastes his tea, that I hope this one is more to his liking. He doesn't add his usual two sugars which seems a good sign. Orange tea. Seville orange, masking the orange-coloured juice from the celandine stalks I had found by the wall near the canal, stalks which had stained my hands and whose odour, as I had snapped the stalks, made me feel nauseous. I had tested the tea myself in an earlier experimental tea ceremony, to be sure of no aftertaste, a small mouthful rapidly spat out. So when I came to prepare Edmund's cup, I had known how many drops of liquid to drip into the bottom before pouring the Seville orange tea on top. In fourteen hours or so he is going to feel extremely ill.

Poor bastard. Sitting there unsuspectingly sipping his tea. I watch his lips purse around the cup before sipping the orange-scented, orange-coloured liquid. He is telling me about his cousin whose wife died in childbirth, six months ago now, and how his cousin is managing with the child that he has been lumbered with. I remember Edmund telling me of this woman's death. I had seen her at a drinks party about a month before she was due to give birth. A tall woman carrying her pregnancy with ease, as if she were not pregnant at all. Although I had met her at least a dozen times in the past, every time we met we were reintroduced and shook hands as if we were complete strangers. I was of no interest to her because I could be of no use to her, neither for her career nor in her social life. Did she actually believe that I did not remember every time I had been introduced to her? Perhaps she did. Had she secretly felt unmemorable herself, too polite to remind me that we had met previously at so-and-so? Perhaps she truly did not remember the occasions that we had been introduced to each other, but I prefer not to think that it is I who am forgettable. I had disliked her. Yet when Edmund had come in one Thursday to tell me of her death I had been upset. Partially because I had seen her as belonging to that breed of Englishwoman that is invincible, but also because I found it difficult to believe that a woman could die in childbirth. Surely not towards the end of the twentieth century, not in the Western world. But they did, apparently, and so had she. This perfectly healthy woman had bled to death while giving birth. Had haemorrhaged and no amount of pumping fresh blood into her could stop it flowing out. So the .doctors had given up and cut her belly open to get the child out.

According to Edmund his cousin is doing very well, looking after the child on his own and is managing splendidly. At this Edmund grimaced before saying that if it had been him he would have gone mad, would be unable to bear the child anywhere near him, let alone be able to hold it. He would be terrified that he would suffocate it or break its neck because it had taken the life of its mother. Surely, he said, a child was meant to be an extension of the love between a man and a woman, not a replacement for one of them. He said that until the death of his cousin's wife he had thought it probable that he would, one day, have children but that now he probably wouldn't. He looked at children with loathing, at pregnant women with disgust, their swollen bellies horrifying him. Imagine, he said, a foetus engorging itself on the food that you digested, like a parasite, growing bigger and bigger, cramping your internal organs, taking you over. I understood his disgust, empathized with his repugnance. As Edmund sipped his tea, I momentarily wished that there was no celandine in it. I'm truly fond of him. But only momentarily.

v

I stretch my legs out from where I have had them tucked underneath me on the sofa. I feel their thirty-three years resisting movement. In my head I am still eighteen, but when I look at my legs throbbing in front of me the extent of my years becomes apparent. Veins and muscles that are ageing and becoming worn and strained signal that I am certainly not as young as I like to think I am. At the moment I feel old, everything has the potential to irritate me, to provoke a tantrum. I look at the books surrounding me on the sofa and floor. How Mary Blandy riles me, while at the same time remaining enticing.

What is it about her that continues to exert such a powerful fascination? It is no exaggeration to say that her contemporaries are obsessed with her. At least thirty texts have been written, some declaring her innocent, others attesting to her guilt. More recent commentators of the case have continued to take up her cause. The perennial fascination with the case seems to stem from the simple fact that she went to the gallows vociferously asserting her innocence. All guilt she firmly placed with her aristocratic lover, Captain the Honourable William Cranstoun. The bizarre thing is that many have tended to take her assertion of innocence at face value, and viewed Mary as little more than a channel for Cranstoun's devious wickedness. Yet it is obvious to me, blatantly so, that throughout her own telling of events *Miss Mary Blandy's Own Account*, she repeatedly contradicts herself in order to be extricated from damning situations and to deny foreknowledge of particular events. She is guilty. Palpably guilty, or so I think.

Outwardly the form of her life is conventional. Dependent upon her father, living within his home until she is found a suitable husband, she inhabits a world of gentle and genteel ease. Educated at home by an adoring mother, Mary is known for her intelligence though at the

39

same time not being considered learned or a bluestocking. She is accomplished at the tasks expected of girls of her class: needlework, drawing, music. Her mornings pass assisting her mother in the sundry details of housekeeping in a staffed house, and her afternoons in visiting and being visited.

If Mary were sitting opposite me now what would we find to say to each other? I who am accomplished at nothing other than bookselling. Might we talk about books and reading and the reading of books? For it seems that she took a particular pleasure in reading, especially the works of Aphra Behn. Had Mary yearned for a life similar to Behn's, one of her own making, a life of adventure and danger? Perhaps she and I are kindred spirits. There she is now, sitting forward in her chair, holding a cup of tea, skirts lifting a little to show the prison leg-irons encasing her slender ankles. I study her long face, highly browed with an aquiline nose. She appears calm, her gaze does not seek sympathy, yet there is something about those eyes, so heavy-lidded, arrogant, disdainful. Daring me to judge her.

Smallpox scars were said to mark her face, but contemporary engravings do not betray them. In one she sits at a desk in her cell in Oxford Castle, quill poised in her left hand. In another she lolls on a grassy bank with Cranstoun, intimately resting her elbow on his shoulder. She regards her viewer in engravings, mezzotints, a sepia drawing, portrayed in the height of fashion. Even when depicted in leg-irons she is made to embody the public's fascination for the 'innocent' beauty fallen into wickedness.

And Cranstoun? What of he who enters her life when she is twenty-six? Cranstoun is the fifth son of a Scottish

Lord and appears highly, highly eligible. Yet few kind words have been said of Cranstoun. He is dismissed as a liar and a cad, a corrupter of innocence, the villain of the piece. Descriptions of Cranstoun do, however, beg the question of what on earth it is that attracts Mary to him. When they met he is in his mid-forties, short, sandy-haired, piggy-eyed, his face disfigured with smallpox scars. In spite of his lack of appeal Mary is not alone in finding him an attractive proposition. In fact, she merely joins the long queue of women who have met the arch-flatterer and succumbed to his honey-tongued words. If Mary perhaps is not the love of his life, there can be little doubt that he becomes hers.

The pair first meet at a garden party in Henley, in the summer of 1746. It is a brief and supposedly inauspicious meeting and the couple were not to meet again for months. Yet such is its intensity that the next time they meet, Cranstoun proposes marriage. Is it love at first sight or does the £10,000 dowry that Mary's father offers act as an enticement to Cranstoun?

In reality, Cranstoun is not free to marry, as he is already possessed of a wife and child who live in Scotland, although he is challenging the legitimacy of this marriage in the Scottish courts. In addition to his wife and child, Cranstoun also keeps a mistress upon whom he has fathered a child, as well as a mistress whom he maintains in London.

By the summer of 1750 Mary was aware of the intricacies of Cranstoun's private life. Yet she remained constant in her declarations of love and desire to marry him. In fact such is the depth of the love that she felt for him that when she is arrested for the poisoning of her father, she is quoted at the trial as saying that she 'declined to assist in bringing Cranstoun to justice, for she considered him as her husband, although the ceremony had not passed between them'.

These are the only words we have from Mary that so much as hint at the intensity of feeling which she harbours for him. She considered him as her husband. Do they imply a verbal contract between the couple, unwitnessed, as Cranstoun is after all still married? More likely, they imply a sexual relationship. Sexual intimacy would not have been unusual. One of the courting rituals of the eighteenth century was the custom of 'bundling' which allowed for physical intimacy but not full sexual intercourse. Given that Mary and Cranstoun's relationship existed over a number of years, many of which, as a potential son-in-law, Cranstoun spent in protracted periods of residence under the Blandy roof, it does not seem unreasonable to suggest that 'bundling' took place. Did they, after Mary's parents retired, go to her room, where she would undress for Cranstoun in the flickering firelight while a maid 'dozed' in a nearby chair – for the etiquette of 'bundling' required the presence of a female witness to observe that the parameters of decency were, to some degree, maintained. Had they lain side by side kissing, touching, exploring each other's bodies?

It would seem so, for in late 1750 Cranstoun is asked to leave Henley after Mr Blandy discovers him in a bedroom with Mary late at night, accompanied by a maid. It will be the last time that he and Mary will ever see each other.

Possibly for the first time, Francis Blandy attended to the intensity of Mary's relationship with Cranstoun, realizing that his daughter is in fact by now a thirty-year-old woman. In the forthcoming months he forbids Mary to so much as correspond with Cranstoun, who has returned to Scotland, and slowly attempts to erase every memory of him from Mary's mind. Superficially she appears acquiescent to her father's commands, but secretly she and Cranstoun are soon back in touch.

How awful the father and daughter relationship must have become. Mary's resentment turns to loathing, her loathing to hatred. She is thirty and believes that her father is obstructing her personal happiness. She views herself on the verge of spinsterhood, doomed to spend the remainder of her years pandering to an old man, seeing herself becoming old, dry, desiccated, sexless. Not through lack of marriage offers but because of her father's financial control over her. For although her father has offered to provide a £10,000 dowry when the appropriate suitor presents himself, applicant after applicant is rebuffed, deemed unsuitable for a variety of reasons. At one point her father takes Mary to Bath for the season, ostensibly to find her a good match. But does he really want his daughter to marry? For after his murder it emerges that he has lied. There has never been a £10,000 dowry for Mary when she marries. Mr Blandy did not have such a sum.

The deception concerning her dowry also ensnared Mary. It seems reasonable to assume that she had come to believe that her father would not consent to a marriage because he did not wish to give her a dowry. She fantasized a life with Cranstoun, a life they had planned in shared whispers between kisses late at night, a life in a world where there is no impediment to their love. A life where Mary has no father and is in possession of £10,000.

In May 1751 Cranstoun sends Mary a package that contains a gift of Scotch pebbles, worn at the time as the height of fashion. Tucked inside the package is an envelope with the words written on the front 'the powder to clean the pebbles with'. The powder is white arsenic. At her trial will Mary state that she believed the powder to be a love philtre that Cranstoun had obtained from a 'cunning woman', and designed to be put into her father's tea to soften his heart towards Cranstoun.

Yet when the adverse effects of the philtre on her father's health become apparent and Mary begins to suspect the love potion, she does not write Cranstoun a damning letter. Rather, her response is to place an even larger dose into her father's food. Subsequently when her father becomes so unwell that the doctor is called, Mary shrugs off the illness as due to heartburn and colic, ailments which he suffers on occasion. It is only following the similar illness of a maid, after she has finished food meant for Francis Blandy, that suspicions are aroused.

Mary attempted to burn the evidence – Cranstoun's letters and the poison – but a quick-witted maid retrieves the debris from the fire and passes it to the doctor who takes it away for analysis. Instead of keeping a discreet distance from Cranstoun, as would have seemed sensible, Mary sends him a letter warning him to take care in writing to her in case his letters go astray. This is immediately intercepted.

In the week that it takes Francis Blandy to die in great agony, Mary is confined to her room and only allowed to visit her father once. Informed of her father's death, Mary initially 'showed no sign of sorrow, compassion, or remorse', according to a contemporary source, but on the day of the coroner's inquest she panicked and attempted to flee. She had every reason to be fearful for the autopsy will find that Francis Blandy has indeed died from arsenic poisoning.

With the findings of the inquest Mary is arrested and sent to Oxford Castle. Imprisoned she is treated with considerable laxity. Waited on by two servants, she takes tea with visitors and walks accompanied in the grounds. It is only when rumours of a possible attempt to smuggle her from prison become known that the authorities decide to take no risks and have her placed in leg-irons. Her trial lasts thirteen hours, culminating in a verdict of guilty and a sentence of death. Cranstoun, who has gone into hiding after her arrest, flees to France at her sentence of death by hanging, where he will die of a tumour only eight months later.

Mary dies in front of a gathering of strangers, still declaring her innocence. A dubious innocence pithily summed up by Walpole when he writes of her: 'As if a woman who would not stick at parricide would scruple a lie.'

From the moment we arrived, Mary said, she knew why Mackie had left and never returned. The house seemed shrouded. Mausoleum-like. Dark. A quiet corner where dead things lived.

Mary had called Mackie's mother after we had buried him. Telephoned her, just as Mackie had left her instructions to do, should anything ever happen to him. His mother had been curt and brief, telling Mary to bring Mackie's death certificate and the child's birth certificate. Proof, Mary supposed, that she was not a fraud, a confidence trickster, out to gain access to an old lady's house and then rob her of her life's savings. Mary understood such precautions, she said. It took us a week in the van to get there, driving slowly and stopping to enjoy the view. Why rush, Mary said. There would be plenty of time to talk to Mackie's mother of his life and to introduce her to her granddaughter.

Mary changed her mind at the gate, one hand hovering above the latch the other enclosing my hand. Looking up the path hemmed in by tall, fir trees to a dark, gloomy verandah, she debated turning and leaving, disappearing, just as Mackie had done twenty-seven years previously. Then the door opened and a big woman, solid, had boomed down the path, to not just stand there but bring the child in. So Mary had. Walked up the garden path past the firs and up the steps to stand on the verandah and then had had to tip her head back to look up to meet the gaze of Mackie's mother. For she was tall, Mary said, the tallest woman she had ever met, six foot at least, and big with it, a solid rectangle of human flesh.

And I? What did I remember of it all? Nothing, it seemed. If I thought hard I could just make out the path with the sentinel firs ensuring that the only option was to move forward, straight towards the door. They sat and had tea, Mackie's mother and Mary, while I was given cordial – lime – which I refused to drink, never having had lime cordial before. I sat with the glass to my mouth, mouth open, teeth hooked on the edge of the glass staring at my feet. One of my less attractive habits, Mary always said.

The adults talked – question and answer was how Mary phrased it – until the past twenty-odd years had been excavated. Then we were invited to stay and Mary had said yes, too nervous to say no, and we had stayed for a month, sleeping in a room that never seemed to grow light. Most days Mary fled, out and about on chores, leaving me in the house which I tremulously explored, coming across room after room no one ever seemed to go into except to dust.

Eventually I found the room that Mackie's mother's mother sat in, positioned by the window, in a plush blue-velvet chair, so she could watch the day pass. When I had tried to sneak away, her head, fragile, egg-like, had swung my way and a whispered come here, girl, had wafted to where I hovered in the doorway. Having been brought up to do as I was told, I did so on this occasion, and stood apprehensively in front of a face so old that it seemed that it could not possibly be alive. Although when the old lady smiled the latticework of lines and wrinkles that comprised her face suddenly fell into place. She asked me to turn around, which I did, then to undress, which I did, and after she had run her eyes over every inch of my bare body, she had nodded, saying good, good and told me to replace my clothes, and then told me I could go.

If I hadn't seen her again a little over a week later, I am unsure how I would have recalled my great-grandmother, but still discovering hidden corners of the house, I stumbled upon her playing the piano, leg pumping, hands flying over the keys. From behind she looked like a young woman such energy did she exude until I caught a glimpse of the side of her face which in this instance resembled a skull, so tightly was the skin moulded to the contours of bone. Horrified, I shrank away, unnoticed.

Later I came to fear that room, would stand in the doorway starting at shadows, certain that the heavy velvet drapes were moving, softly swaying to entice me, coax me, into their folds, to slowly enwrap me until I was hidden and trapped and unable to breath. I would stand shaking with anxiety, unable to move until, finally, I would tear myself away and run, legs pounding, out into the sunshine where I would stand panting, eyes glued on the back door just to make sure that whatever-it-was had not followed me. I don't know where it came from that fear, just that one day it was there and it never went away and I could never again enter that room where my great-grandmother sat to play the piano.

At the end of the month Mary and I left the house and, indeed, Mary had been out running errands, as she had said, and had not just abandoned me to those dark rooms. During that month Mary had been finding a house for us to live in, a decent distance from Mackie's mother, who had provided the funds from what would have been Mackie's inheritance if he had lived. It seemed more sensible to put the money to use now when it was needed rather than to leave it in the bank. It was an ordinary house on one level with six rooms and with five acres to plant fruit and vegetables. I loved the house, how I loved it. No hidden corners, just big, bright, square rooms with a front and a back verandah. A white picket fence, a garden path leading to the front verandah then through a screen door straight into the living room; the room to the left was Mary's bedroom, from living room through to the eat-in kitchen and the room to the left of that was my bedroom. Then back into the kitchen and down two steps and on the right a spare room and on the left the bathroom-cum-laundry, then out through the screen door onto the back verandah and down ten steps to the grass – for the house was built on a bit of a slope – and the clothes-line and the garden, and the sheds and the chicken run and then fields rolling away and away. Fields that Mary planted with all manner of seeds and trees: apple, plum, pear and cherry trees, spinach, potatoes, sweetcorn, peas, beans, onions, tomatoes, leeks, zucchini, aubergine, pumpkin, cauliflower, cabbage, brussel sprouts, strawberries, rhubarb, watermelon, and still there was room for a grapevine. But that was some time later. Before we could move in the house needed renovating – the reason Mackie's mother had got such a bargain was that it was all a bit ramshackle. The rooms needed painting and the roof leaked and the sewage pipes were not connected, the toilet was an outhouse and men in a truck came and emptied the can twice a week. I asked why we didn't go in the garden and provide some fertilizer, to which Mary replied that we lived in a house now and people who lived in houses did not shit in their garden. But Mary loathed the outhouse as much as I did – and a proper toilet was her first priority in renovating the house.

Around the house itself Mary planted an English garden with daffodils, bluebells and lilac – purple and white – for springtime and masses upon masses of honeysuckle and roses for summer. Yellow and white roses that climbed up and around the front verandah, growing over the window of Mary's bedroom and obscuring the light, while housing nests of spiders that would scuttle through the house days before a rainfall. It is the only house that I have ever lived in. My rooms over the bookshop are not quite the same. Home, but not.

Over the years we visited Mackie's mother and her mother irregularly, two or three times a year. The two died within a year of each other and the shrouded house was sold after Mackie's sisters had finished quarrelling over their mother's and grandmother's jewellery and knick-knacks. Squabbling like magpies, Mary said, only with magpies it was one for sorrow and two for joy, but those two had never, ever, been a joy to anyone, not even to their mother.

I subsequently discovered by looking at the dates in the family Bible that my great-grandmother had been one hundred and three when she had died in her sleep one heat-smothered afternoon, in her chair by the window. My grandmother, Mackie's mother, had died a year later, not quietly at home but in hospital, her liver devoured by cancer, drugged on morphine but still screaming in agony, tied to the bed for her own safety, her daughters had said, as they rifled her wardrobes and drawers, closets and cupboards, saying that they hoped never again to see anyone suffer the way their mother had.

What had these two women, my grandmother and her mother – whom I had only known as old and fearsome in their decay – shared in the passage of years that ticked by in that house? How close had they been, mother and daughter? When I try to imagine my great-grandmother as a young wife holding Mackie's mother in her arms, my mind goes blank. Was the house dark even then or had it been light-filled? When had it become shadowed, who had planted all those trees, perhaps for shade, but only successful in expelling, repelling light.

Had it been Mackie's mother? She who had buried two of her sons and then had the third run away from her to join a foreign war. To fight for a country that had happily sent her forebears over in convict ships, manacled in leg-irons, not giving a damn about whether they lived or died only that they were out of the way on the other side of the world. Her son fighting for the mother country? Her son fighting for the king? Be damned, she had told him, if you go, don't ever come back. So he hadn't.

How often had his mother thought of him, wondered whether he was alive or dead, her last remaining son, born four months after the death of her husband in a shooting accident, which left her with four children and one on the way. Had she thanked God that she still had her own mother without whom she would never have managed? Her mother whom she adored and in whose absence she would certainly have taken the shotgun and killed all the children and then herself. For it was her mother and her mother's piano playing, which reminded her of her own childhood, that had kept her going after her husband's death.

I don't remember my grandmother. Not an iota of memory do I have of her. Not even in my memory's memory. How many times had I been left in her company? Yet I can't recall a thing about her. Not her voice, nor her hair, nor her smell. I solely remember the stories that I had been told by Mary, but these are not my memories, they belong to Mary. Apparently Mackie's mother had liked me. According to Mary, during the weeks that we had stayed I had accompanied my grandmother when she went to play bridge with her cronies, every other afternoon. I had sat quietly in the corner of the sofa tucked up with a book while they played, and then when the old girls had finished they would sit and drink sherry and gossip and I also would be allowed to sip a small sherry but only after I had sung them a song. Mackie's mother told Mary this story every time we visited, requesting a photograph to be able to show her bridge pals, who never failed to ask after me, her granddaughter.

When I think of my grandmother, I think of her in a photograph that I have, where she is about the same age as I was when I made my confirmation. Euphrosyne is sitting on the grass, knees curled up underneath her and she is holding a book which it appears she is about halfway through reading. Her hair is swept up and held in place by a large shiny bow and she's laughing at the camera, a face-splitting grin, eyes screwed up, laughing at whomever is taking her picture.

Whenever I look at the picture my heart lurches momentarily then continues sluggishly. For I know what life holds in store for this girl, I know how she will outlive her husband and sons and finally die in agony a year after her own mother. I know that her granddaughter will be unable to remember her even though she clenches her grandmother's blue glass rosary beads in the palm of her hand, squeezing hard, as if the pressure of beads upon flesh will trigger a memory.

I look at Euphrosyne and ache for her, a longing that emanates from the pit of my stomach. I need to know what the book is that she is reading, if it is a book that I have read myself. I want to whisper come back, talk to me, just for a moment, tell me the answers to all the questions that I have. Instead my fingertip touches her face, covering it, concealing the face of the girl who laughs in the sunshine. Then, carefully, I put the photograph away.

THREE

Edmund has stayed the night. No, it's not like that. Nothing like that at all. Edmund and I have not done that for some time. Thrice we slept together. Had sex, that is, neither good nor bad, just inadequate, a lot of hard work for very little return. We are too compatible, Edmund and I, to find each other sexually stimulating. There is no danger, no frisson, no temptation. We are both too ordinary. As bog-standard, as middle-of-the-road as each other, we do not engage in the required way that induces libidinousness. Who knows what it is that provokes an accelerated pulse? I, certainly, do not. I don't seem to have a type — actually, that isn't strictly true, I do have a type but they are never interested in me. That, I know.

It's not that Edmund isn't fanciable, because he is. Lovely hair that is just a bit too long, brown eyes, long-fingered hands, strong wrists. He appears desirable when dressed, but the minute that he takes off his shirt it is difficult not to avert one's gaze. He has a writer's posture, round-shouldered, which is fine when his shoulders are draped in clothing but when not it merely reveals a sunken chest with no muscle to speak of, flaccid, spongy. Removal of his trousers is even worse: bony knees, bony arse, cold bony feet, skin the colour of pumice. That particular, peculiar colour that germinates under a sticking plaster wrapped around a finger for a week, which upon removal displays skin that is white, spongy. Edmund is like that all over. All over. But when he is dressed he is desirable, those limbs hidden beneath shirts, jackets and long trousers.

In bed Edmund and I made each other feel inadequate. It occurs sometimes, out of the blue, whatever urge that leads one to remove one's clothes suddenly evaporates. We gave up after attempt number three left Edmund wilted and me dissatisfied. I had sat propped up against the pillows, arms folded against my breasts as Edmund apologized repeatedly and I had tried to contain and not betray my resentment, eventually sending him off to make a pot of tea in order to be rid of him. Taking his clothes with him he had dressed in the kitchen and then carried the tea back to bed, perching his clothed self on the edge and handing me a cup while studiously avoiding my eyes. Listening to the rustle of his shirt as he raised the cup to his lips, my anger dissipated. I desired him once more and noticing his dismayed expression I wondered if he had sensed that I found his unclothed body repellent, found the thought of his white skin touching mine nauseating. Now that he was dressed I could be magnanimous and I rubbed his trousered leg and told him that truly it didn't matter. Relief flooded his face and he had muttered something I didn't catch and leant towards me repeatedly brushing my curls back from my face, his palm rasping in its encounter against my forehead. Curling his body to face away from me he had lain his head in between my chin and my shoulder. I rested my jaw on his head, my hand rubbing his back, fingers fiddling with the lumps of his vertebrae which when felt through fabric felt interesting, something to be encountered more closely.

But that was some years ago. Edmund stayed last night because occasionally he does and we slept together. Shared my bed in which we slept. He is still upstairs asleep. He had stayed and stayed after I had closed the bookshop, so I suggested going to the pub. Instead we reached a compromise with red wine and take-away pizza. By the time Edmund seemed ready to leave it was more sensible that he stayed and so we retired, I taking the window side and Edmund near the edge, our usual sleeping positions.

Half asleep I could hear him moaning, just a little, then burping, then moaning again. He whimpered that he felt sick, drawing out each word in a small voice. Silence. Shifting to lie on his back he drew deep breaths which he held, as if in the hope that an influx of oxygen would quell his heaving stomach. A finger poking me in the back – and again. I feigned sleep. He leant and whimpered in my ear, I feel sick. Keeping my eyes firmly closed I muttered to go to the lavatory. Then he sat up, groaning, and suddenly I feared that he would vomit in the bed, on the bedcovers. As he swung his legs to the floor he shouted accusingly that he was going to be sick, almost as if he knew that it was my fault. I listened to his feet padding quickly to the bathroom and the click as the light was switched on, then his heave and the splatter of lumps of undigested pizza mixed with wine as it slopped into the toilet bowl. Silence. Another heave; more vomit. The toilet flushed, but he remained in the bathroom. I turned onto my other side so that I could see the bathroom door. Then in rapid succession another three heaves which emptied his stomach. I imagined him on his knees in my green flannel pyjamas, the ridges of the tiles coldly cutting into his skin. I could hear the tap running, for him to rinse the taste of vomit from his mouth I suppose, to remove those particles that are like porridge, which always remain clinging to one's teeth after vomiting. As the bathroom light flicked off he expelled a long strangled fart that echoed around the small bathroom, bouncing off the walls. Pad, pad, pad, pad, and he was back in bed, laying his drained body down, shaking considerably. I pulled the covers up to his chin and in a tiny voice he told me I've been sick. I brushed his fringe back from his forehead which was cold and damp and inquired whether I could get anything for him. He moved his head no, he thought he'd go to sleep now. I murmured that it must have been the pizza and he turned his face away from me saying that he didn't want to think about it.

Within the hour he was up again, then again, and again. I must admit I was astonished at how much his scrawny carcass contained to void. By the morning he was a shapeless mass huddled under the covers, napping fitfully, holding his arms around his stomach with his knees drawn chinwards.

I opened the bookshop as usual, behaving much as I normally did. Every hour I placed on the door the back-in-10-minutes sign so I could go upstairs and check how he was faring. I need not have bothered for he slept through the morning until late afternoon. I closed the shop a little early, business had been brisk – there is nothing like a back-in-10-minutes sign to have the punters queueing – and I felt justified in closing early. I was in good form that day, I could have sold a Bible to the devil. Everyone who came in the door left having purchased a book.

Feeling pleased with myself I ran Edmund a bath and then propped him on the sofa while I threw open the bedroom window to clear the putrid stink of vomit. Downstairs he rested, wan and exhausted, but not too unwell to play the mother-me game. He wanted tomato soup for supper and when I didn't have the brand that he liked he demanded that I go out and buy some. When I whined about having had a long day in the shop, he sulked that he wasn't hungry anyway, so he would go without.

Not realizing that he had all my sympathy, as much as I had to offer, Edmund had had to test it, couldn't resist pushing the limits, thereby ruining it. He sat and sulked. It must be Heinz tomato soup accompanied by buttered toast cut into soldiers, or nothing at all. He couldn't possibly have Campbell's soup for they had slaughtered some branch of his family at Glen Coe. He had never had Campbell's soup and was not going to now. I looked at him and could very easily imagine the child he had been, spitefully thinking that it was no wonder his mother had gone mad and had to be locked away. But that was cruel and unnecessary and, feeling remorse for the thought, I capitulated. Heinz soup it was. It would be a relief to get away from the silly bastard. My parting quip, which his expression conveyed he found in poor taste, was that I might return with a pizza for myself.

Once out into the night I found it hard to stop walking. The wind had dropped and a thick fog had appeared since I had closed the shop. How thrilling I found it. The obfuscation of the ordinary. The streets were relatively quiet and the lamps shone their alien orange glow through the mantle of fog. Yes, I loved hot weather but the fog excited me. I walked to the park and found my way to the inner circle, footsteps echoing. I might be the only person on earth. Walking in a fog was perhaps the closest sensation I could get to what it might possibly be like to be blind, to have no sense at all of what was in front of my eyes. I ran my fingers along the railings. The condensation numbed my fingertips and formed into perfect droplets before falling to the ground. My ears quivered at the slightest sound, the fog dripping from tree branches menaced me, sounding like footsteps slowly stalking my footsteps.

So, the celandine had worked. Had more than worked. If the dose had been any higher it might have been fatal. I would need to be careful. Edmund was not unrobust, but his heart might not take the strain, or his kidneys, or his liver. How awful that would be: Edmund alive but incapacitated. An invalid, from kidney failure or a heart attack. I have to admit to myself that I am unsure of what I am doing, and use for guidance the rule that less is more. One drop instead of three next time.

Poor Edmund. Did he really deserve to suffer in this way? Just because his book infuriated me. Just because he was a Maskelyne didn't mean that he hadn't had his share of misfortune and unhappiness.

Had his mother loved him? He'd always told me that she had said that by having him she had done her duty and that was that. She had come from good Indian Colonial stock, Indian born and bred she had liked to say. Then when he was eight she had gone mad and been put away in an asylum. A rather nice one, Edmund added, but still an asylum. Two years later she had been released but her illness had recurred, and despite all the drugs and the electric shock treatment she had grown worse until finally she was unable to recognize her family. She was still alive. Edmund rarely spoke of her, certainly never went to see her. She was still a young woman, had turned eighteen on the day of her marriage and given birth to Edmund a little over a year later. His mother would only be fifty-odd now and could, probably would, live for decades more.

Edmund's father, a poet, had been twice her age, and after his wife's incarceration in a mental home, had gone to live in Malta, where he had died while Edmund was still a teenager. He had hardly known either of his parents, he said. Most of his time was spent at boarding school, and his holidays at the family home in Suffolk where Hermione's autocratic presence reigned. He had loathed his grandmother, who had taunted him that his mother's bad blood coursed through his veins. Imagine growing up with that, I thought, fagging at school and at home a grandmother who thought it amusing to tell other members of the family that Edmund was slightly bertie, just like his mother.

He had had no friendly presence at all. His grandfather had so disliked his own wife that he had lived in Egypt where, a brigadier, he had been killed in a skirmish during the war. Every other year he had returned to the house in Suffolk, and following a two-week visit would return to Egypt. After every visit Hermione was pregnant, so at least the brigadier was doing his duty. And over the span of twelve years she had given birth to five girls and a boy, Laurence, Edmund's father. After her husband's death in Egypt Hermione forbade him to be spoken about. It was when he hadn't appeared for his biennial visit that she had found out about his death, for the brigadier had had himself listed as having no next of kin and left his few effects to one of his colleagues in Cairo. Cremated, with his ashes scattered to the desert winds, there was little Hermione could do, apart from erecting an Egyptian-style obelisk in the grounds of the house, amongst the rhododendrons, engraved with the brigadier's name.

ii

I have driven Edmund home through another thickening fog. Today he was a little more sturdy, well enough to have taken himself home this morning, instead of malingering on my sofa, browsing through my books, disarranging them, battering them, tossing them to the floor. How someone who is meant to love books can treat them so badly, with such disrespect, is beyond me. His books are in a state beyond repair, beyond despair. He cracks their spines as he opens them, writes in their margins in ink, bends down the corner of a page to mark a place. Unforgivable.

We ate together before he left. His favourite, roast pork with roast vegetables, cooked by himself as a thank you for my kindness. As a treat for him I basted his carrots with a little warm honey, and added the merest droplet of celandine. Tomorrow he will call me and tell me that he has a stomach-ache, that he has been nauseous but not sick, and surmise that he has a stomach bug; possibly he has picked up some germ that is doing the rounds, for it is that time of year, is it not?

Tomorrow, Sunday, how I would like to keep the shop closed for the afternoon but I cannot afford not to open. I am also behind in my cataloguing due to Edmund's presence over the past couple of days. This particular boxful of women are a whole different breed to the parricides. These women are cunning, these women got away with their crimes even though they were suspected. I wonder how many women over the centuries have got away without a whiff of suspicion. How many women wielded their murderous power through another, a lover for example. How many who devised sinister schemes that involved cold-blooded risk-taking, where the financial stakes were high, and the results could, and did, end in violence and death. Women who then walked away to carry on life as normal while their lover went to the gallows.

On an ordinary winter's morning in London, in January 1699, John Sayer, a member of the landed gentry, had married Mary Nevil, a woman of similar station. It is a first marriage for them both, a marriage that is, I presume, arranged in the usual fashion of the time. Within weeks of their marriage Mary has banished her husband from the marital bed and, not only is she taking little care to hide her disgust of him, she has taken to declaring in public that she finds him abhorrent. This is the inauspicious beginning to a marriage that will end thirteen years later with the murder of John Sayer at the hands of one of his wife's lovers and culminate in the trial that will be the *cause célèbre* of 1713.

What had happened throughout those thirteen years? They were years of increasing misery for Sayer and extraordinary debauchery and deception for Mary Sayer. For Sayer, it seems, was willing to tolerate Mary's sexual exploits, which encompassed conquests of his own friends. For thirteen years he was to endure her disregard and spiteful temper, manifested in public by her denigration of himself. Years during which Mary is gradually ostracized by her female friends, whose pity and sympathy regarding her husband's situation turn to uncomprehending bewilderment. It is a relationship that ebbs and flows with Mary's viciousness, swelling time and again, but never actually breaking. Not, at least, until Mary found a lover, Richard Noble, who is willing to be her pawn, who will become ensnared in the lies she tells about her husband, and will finally kill him.

At six o'clock on the morning of Friday, March 13th, 1713, the trial for the murder of John Sayer commenced.

Richard Noble was charged with wilful stabbing. Mary, along with her mother, was charged with aiding and abetting. On these indictments all three pleaded not guilty. That Noble struck Sayer with a sword causing 'a wound the length of half an inch and a depth of six inches' as a contemporary document states, in the presence of Mary and her mother was not doubted. However, Noble's plea is one of self-defence.

Finally having established a jury, after the three accused had gone through a lengthy process of jury challenging, the first witness was called and the tragic tale began to unfold. One of Mary's maids tells how her mistress had attempted to poison her husband, conspiring to make the maid her accomplice. Another maid corroborates this evidence and tells of Mary's repeated affairs throughout the marriage. Affairs which had resulted in at least two bastard children when attempts at abortion had failed. Witness after witness testifies to Mary's repeated animosity toward her husband, to her flaunting her lovers, and to her final entanglement with Noble, who had been her husband's lawyer and business adviser. As I read through each witness's testimony it became apparent that although it had been Noble who had dealt the fatal blow, it was indisputable that it had been at Mary's instigation.

But why had it happened? I do not understand why John Sayer had allowed his marriage to reach this point. There were ways of dealing with the shortcomings of a marriage – aside from giving Mary the thrashing she clearly deserved – Sayer could, quite simply, have divorced her. Curiously, though, it was a life he seemed to tolerate, allowing his blind adoration for his whorish wife – or his masochism – to overwhelm his better judgement. Again and again she exposed him to public humiliation and with monotonous regularity he forgave her behaviour, so that it leaves us with little doubt that he condoned it.

I leaf through the seven books on the case hoping for a portrait of her, but there are none. Was she of such astounding beauty as to win his forbearance, or was he just simple-minded? I look around the bookshop at my clutch of Sunday browsers, all of whom are in couples, some married, no doubt, some not. They call each other across the room to point out a book, to show an illustration, a line of text. It is easy to spot the potential duos for the man preens, flaunting his knowledge, providing a potted lesson on whatever-it-is that he is looking at, to his companion, who listens.

Why is it never a woman who expounds upon a subject for a silent companion? Why are women never the ones to flick open a book and say oh look, dah di dah di dah di dah? What do these silent women get from these diarrhoea-mouthed men? A paid meal? Sex? Companionship? What is going on in their heads while they listen to an exposition on some play, a piece of prose, a photograph, a painting? Most likely they are plotting the baby-in-the-pram two years down the line. The pram which will clutter up my shop on their future visits.

Truly, who knows what these women want from these men. Do they know themselves? When on occasion they buy a book, walking out hand in hand, I visualize them some years from now arguing over who is going to have it now that they will soon no longer be together, arguing over who actually paid for it, or perhaps not caring, throwing it into a box of items to be disposed of, to be sold, so that it wends its way back to me, often with the price still pencilled inside in my own handwriting. Then I smile and think fondly of the couple gone their separate ways. It is those who remain together year after year who are the liars, the frauds, the compromisers. They are the ones not to be trusted.

And, delightful Mary Sayer, what of her? What right have I to be so self-righteously moralistic about her? I am, after all, poisoning Edmund. But Mary and I are not sisters in crime, for she used a man to commit her dirty deed. She was unable to make that final leap of the imagination and take her life, and someone else's, into her own hands. This is why I feel justified in disdaining her.

Richard Noble's statements portray her as a consummate manipulator and inveterate liar. Mary's hatred of her husband reached such a pathological extreme that she refused all contact with her first child on the grounds that it resembled its father.

Eventually John Sayer consents to give her an official separation in which he places lands in trust for her and further provides her with a generous annuity. Despite this, during his absences abroad on business she pillages his residence of money and furniture and then proceeds to take sanctuary in the Mint – a notorious stronghold of thieves and criminals of all types – where she cannot be arrested. Accompanying her are her mother and Richard Noble. For Sayer, unable to reappropriate his property, it must have seemed the final indignity. But worse was to follow when he was presented with four hundred pounds in outstanding debts for goods which Mary and Noble had charged to his account.

Discovering Mary's place of residence in the Mint, John Sayer arrives at the house where she is lodged, accompanied by two constables who are in turn accompanied by half a dozen assistants. Mary, her mother, and Noble have been at lunch when Sayer lays hold of the door and pulls it open. Within minutes he is dead, stabbed by Noble.

In his testimony Noble states that he had heard shouting in the hall and that he believed that the house was being overrun by a gang of thieves. Knowing, he declares, that it was his duty to protect the ladies he had drawn his sword. When the door had been wrenched open he had not stopped to look who was there. Not at any time, he insists, had he been aware that it was John Sayer. This must be a falsehood, for the constables reported that Sayer, from the minute he had entered the building, had shouted for Mary, a voice which certainly she, if not Noble, would have recognized.

Noble, in his own version of events, wrote that he believed that Sayer had 'used his Lady most barbarously, that he beat her, called her names, and had given her a foul Disease'. Stories no doubt spun by Mary which he foolishly believed. Or so he said. For Richard Noble was something of a ladies' man, always choosing women wealthy enough to fund his carefree life.

But not even Mary's money or, more precisely, Mary's access to John Sayer's money can save Noble from the gallows, despite the twenty lawyers and thirty solicitors comprising his council, paid for by Mary. For when the jury returns their verdict Noble is found guilty, while Mary and her mother are acquitted. Mary is so overjoyed at her own escape that her solicitors reprimand her in full view of the court for betraying her lack of concern for Noble, who has received the death sentence.

Some days later Noble is hanged. Deservedly, perhaps, for it isn't possible to deny his central role in the murder, whether he was under Mary's malign influence or not. Neither Mary nor her mother attend his execution or funeral. They have returned to live in the Mint, at the very house, the very rooms, where John Sayer had been slain.

Ushering the last people out of the shop I lock the door, then switch off the lights and sit back in my chair. The shop in darkness, following a day of bustle, is how I am most fond of it. My eyes graze the shelves imagining the remaining books, dwelling on the gaps, velvety dark spaces waiting to be filled with another book. I spend an hour, maybe more, imagining some of the homes that my books have gone to, picturing front rooms and bookshelves, books on bedside tables placed near lamps, books tossed forgotten into a corner. At some point in my musings I fall asleep.

iv

Edmund telephones. He won't be in to see me today, he is poorly. Has been poorly since he last saw me when he was so sick. He exaggerates the pronouncing of the word 'so'; drawing out the 'o', his tone underlines the word at least twice. He hasn't been vomiting but he is continuously nauseous and queasy. Yes, he is eating but only small amounts at a time. He has broken out in strange bumps, like mosquito bites, on his arms and his legs. His doctor thinks that he has eaten something to which he has had an allergic reaction; he has given him a lotion to stop the itching of the bumps and told him to drink a lot of water to flush whatever–it–is from his system.

I raise my eyebrow as he continues talking down the phone. He tells me about the bad dreams he has been having in which I feature. In the dream he stands in the middle of a cornfield and I am walking towards him clothed in white; he knows that it is me even though there is nothing about the woman walking towards him that resembles me. As I approach him he suddenly notices a smell, worse than an overripe Camembert smell, a corpse stench he says, although he doesn't believe he has ever smelt a rotting corpse and asks me if I have. I tell him to get on with the dream. As I get closer he notices that my face is black and in my hands I am holding a white cat and as I lift the cat to my face he sees that actually it isn't a cat at all but an enormous white mouse. Then my mouth opens as if I am asking him a question but he can't hear what I am asking and as he opens his mouth to say that he can't hear me, the white mouse becomes a fat white worm and slides into his mouth and down into his belly where he can feel it moving around and as it moves further down into his gut his stomach becomes distended and I reach out my black deformed hands, which are trembling, and place them on his stomach and the trembling moves down through him to his legs, down to his feet and into the earth which begins to tremble as if there were going to be an earthquake.

What do I make of that, he asks me. I laugh down the phone – my usual expelling of air down my nostrils – and I say that I think that he is a wee bit anxious that he was sick in front of me not too long after we had the conversation about his cousin's wife who had died in childbirth. He says that yes, that was what he had deduced as well. We chat for a while longer, then I make the excuse that I have customers to attend to although the shop is empty. As I gaze into space my mind chews upon the fact that Edmund's subconscious suspects me already.

In 1775 one of the most dramatic forgery trials of the entire eighteenth century took place, a trial for which the evidence rested on the statements of a woman named Margaret Caroline Rudd. As I begin to catalogue the books on the Perreau trial I am slightly confused. What is a trial for forgery doing in a collection of books on women criminals? In the trial Margaret has admitted forging the bond, but under duress, for she has had a knife held to her throat by her lover, Daniel Perreau. As I read my way through the documents I forget that I am meant to be cataloguing, I forget the humming computer. I read.

So antagonistic and potentially riotous is the crowd – some 30,000 in all – that gathers in January 1776 to witness the hanging for forgery of twin brothers Daniel and Robert Perreau, that three hundred constables are drafted in to keep the peace. It turns out, however, to be a peaceable protest at what was perceived to be a terrible miscarriage of justice. A petition for clemency delivered to George III by Robert's wife has been refused although it had been signed by seventy-eight bankers and merchants. Joining hands Daniel and Robert go to their death declaring their innocence.

For five years Margaret Rudd had been living with Daniel Perreau as his common-law wife. Throughout the years of their relationship, which produced three children, Margaret often arrives home with large sums of money which, she informs Daniel, are gifts from two of her relatives, William and James Adair. From the beginning of their liaison Margaret has convinced Daniel that she is related to some of the most noble families in

Scotland and Ireland. The truth was more banal: Margaret had been born into humble beginnings in northern Ireland, but because of unreliable stories she had overheard as a child concerning the parentage of one of her grandmothers, Margaret had convinced herself that she was descended from noble Scots blood, and subsequently gave herself airs and graces befitting a girl of aristocratic descent. Almost certainly these delusions of grandeur contributed to her subsequent behaviour.

For the truth is that Margaret is an imposter. The large sums of money which she presents to Daniel are not generously endowed by well-wishing relatives but instead derived from her earnings as a high-class prostitute. Her wealthy clients who lavish money and gifts upon her include the politician John Wilkes and, prior to meeting Daniel, Margaret had maintained three different lodgings for the purpose of prostitution. But there is an added dimension to her character which makes her particularly dangerous to be associated with: she is an adept forger. Throughout what would become the final year of her relationship with Daniel, 1774–1775, she proficiently forges bonds amounting to a grand total of £72, 250, all forged in the name of her so-called relative, William Adair.

Wondering how much that is today, I get up to see whether I have a copy of Roy Porter's book on the eighteenth century. I flick through the book once, then twice, only to realize that his note for supplying a 'rough and ready' approximation is right at the front of the book. Porter suggests multiplying by eighty, which I do scratching away on a piece of paper. Just then I am interrupted by a customer's voice saying that he hasn't seen anyone doing sums on paper for years. I smile, thinking of all those wasted afternoons at school struggling with logarithm tables and algebraic equations. At least I don't need a till in the shop; I just add up the prices of books in my head or on a piece of paper, keeping my cash tin in a drawer of the desk. Taking my customer's money and putting his book in a carrier bag I maintain my smile as I hand it to him while thinking, now sod off and leave me alone. I start my calculations again and sit back in my chair as it sinks into my brain that in the course of one year alone Margaret forged bonds to the sum of what, in today's currency, is six million pounds.

I open a book to look at her picture, an engraving done in 1775 when she was held in Bridewell Prison on forgery charges. She appears to be a kittenish beauty. Bejewelled, begowned. Her hair in the elaborate pyramid style of the time. How, I wonder, did this delicate, fragile-looking beauty manage to have a single deviant thought, let alone plan a massive forgery, not once, but over and over again? But thinking again, I'm not so surprised, for don't we all know someone like her, kittenish, pretty, vapid, who when crossed is mean and cruel? They are always tiny, these women, with little-girl faces and the sweetest of smiles. They are women with no women friends, but that doesn't matter for they are only interested in men and men find them adorable.

Yet I wonder at Margaret Rudd's self-assurance, her ability to weave not one lie but a whole web of lies and to maintain them under pressure in a courtroom, never once letting the mask slip. Who exactly was she? What had led to her astounding career as a forger? I don't know. I never will know. Margaret's version of events *Facts, or a Plain and Explicit Narrative of the Case of Mrs*

Rudd as Related by Herself is anything but. As I read through it I am astonished at its unashamed nonsense. She presents herself as a pathetic victim, obscuring herself in a text whose sole purpose is to gratify and appease an eighteenth-century public's convictions about women's passivity.

The factual details that I stitch together are scarce. Following her parents' death while she is still a child, she is sent to boarding school but is expelled quite soon afterwards for misconduct with a servant. At fifteen she elopes and has to be forcibly returned to her grandmother's home, and by the age of seventeen she has married Valentine Rudd and is living in London. It isn't long before the marriage goes awry quite simply because Valentine is unable to provide Margaret with the luxuries that she craves. As the outstanding debts escalate it is inevitable that Valentine's inability to pay will cause him to be thrown into a debtor's prison. With her husband in prison and no possibility of an income Margaret turns to prostitution to support herself, bestowing her favours upon whomever bids the most for them. Two years later she encounters Daniel Perreau and concocts the story that she is in hiding from her husband, a drunkard, who has viciously beaten her on innumerable occasions, to such a degree that she fears for her life.

Throughout his own narrative of the case Daniel Perreau insists that he knew nothing of Margaret's reputation as a whore, but I find this difficult to believe. He was given at least one opportunity to find out. Once when Margaret was away, ostensibly visiting her aristocratic family in Scotland, Daniel received a series of anonymous letters which insinuated that Margaret was not the person she presented herself to be, naming her dishonest and disreputable, but levelling no particular charge. Other letters requested a sum of money in payment for relaying a secret of consequence. Daniel would have done well to have taken more notice of these letters, for they might have saved his life.

The truth was that he does not wish to know, does not wish to enquire too deeply into where the funds are coming from, which is unsurprising considering the lavish lifestyle that they maintain, a lifestyle towards which he has made little financial contribution. An account showing Daniel's cellar records for one summer alone shows that the household consumed 729 bottles of champagne and wine. Born into some wealth, Daniel had squandered his inheritance, had been a declared bankrupt, and was known throughout London as a 'needy sharper', that is, a professional cheat at the gaming tables. He seems to have been generally held in low esteem, some people even loathed him, but while it was believed that he would turn a blind eye to Margaret's whoring so as to live off the proceeds, few believed that he would be involved in forgery.

Margaret's game is discovered when two astute bankers, named Drummond, notice that the signature on a bond does not match the usual signature. Robert Perreau, Daniel's twin, has agreed as a favour to cash it for Margaret, a kindness for which he would subsequently be hanged. Unfortunately, the Drummonds are the bankers of William Adair in whose name the bond has been forged. The Drummonds request that the bond be left with them until the signature could be verified. Robert acquiesces.

One can imagine Margaret's panic when Robert informs her of this turn of events, but very coolly she bluffs it out. On the following day they are all asked to meet at the home of William Adair – Margaret, Daniel, Robert and the Drummonds. At this point it is important to remember that throughout the entirety of her relationship with Daniel, Margaret has claimed kinship with Adair – he is the one supposedly funding their exorbitant lifestyle. I can well guess what Daniel must have thought as William Adair states that not only does he have no connection with Margaret, but he has, in fact, never met her before.

As Margaret would have known only too well that this would happen, she must have plotted her next move in advance, for she kept a tight rein on the proceedings. She requests a private audience with the Drummonds and proceeds to confess that she had forged the bond, convincing them by writing on a piece of paper the name of William Adair. It is identical to the signature on the bond and satisfied the Drummonds that Margaret had committed the forgery. This incriminating piece of evidence is then burned. When Margaret and the Drummonds rejoin Adair and the Perreau brothers, they agree that the matter shall go no further.

But then Robert Perreau panics. He feared for his reputation. An apothecary, he diligently ran a prosperous business patronized by the gentry and nobility. If rumour were to get around that he had been involved in a suspected forgery his business might be destroyed. Believing Daniel to be innocent and under the malign influence of Margaret he brings a charge against her for forgery. Both Margaret and Robert are then brought before a magistrate to whom the affair seems of such complexity that he commits them both to Bridewell Prison to await further examination. The following day Daniel is arrested and joins them there. A few days later, the brothers are charged with forgery and committed for trial.

Margaret, meanwhile, is given bail, released and admitted as 'an evidence'. Highly unorthodox this, not that I would have known but for the note pencilled in the margin by a diligent previous reader, disclosing that the person being admitted as an evidence had to have confessed to committing a crime in the first place. Margaret, not having confessed, is not in a position to be called as 'an evidence'. Even more astonishing, she is never asked to give evidence in either Daniel or Robert's trial. So, when the private discussion that she has had with the Drummonds is made public by them at the trial, Margaret, as canny and as cunning as ever, concocts the story of Daniel holding a knife to her throat and forcing her to forge the signature. This will put a seal on the brothers' fate, despite the fact that at the trial witness after witness exposes Margaret as a cold-blooded liar. One of her staff will testify, for instance, that it is Margaret herself who has written a series of fictitious letters, supposedly from William Adair, that always presaged the forging of a bond. In spite of the evidence Daniel and Robert are found guilty and sentenced to death.

To appease the enormous public anger at what was clearly a miscarriage of justice, Margaret is brought to trial on a separate forgery charge. She is, it is reported in the press, demure and composed during the proceedings, even when one of her maids testifies that when she had visited Margaret in prison, her former mistress had offered her money to lie, writing down a set of instructions for her to swear to when questioned in court. Despite such incriminating evidence the jury still brought in a verdict of not guilty.

While imprisoned she had published her *Facts* pertaining to the case and, always one step ahead, it almost certainly helped sway the jury towards her acquittal. Margaret presents herself as the archetypal passive woman swept up in male connivances, a woman whose only real concern is for her children. Page after page, her victimized tone does not vary. Some sections of the press respond by continuing to vilify her:

> Mrs Rudd...slipped through the hangman's fingers, and being let loose on the public is going about like the devil, seeing whom she can devour, it is necessary that the unwary are cautioned to be on their guard against the hellish machinations of such a monster of iniquity for whom no name can be too severe, nor punishment too great.

Strong words, but she seems to have had no conscience at all. Icicle-hearted, sparing no thought for the lover she had sent to the gallows, nor his innocent brother, she resumed her previous lifestyle, moving from one aristocratic lover to another, all of whom kept her in the affluence she presumed her right.

Quite soon after we moved into our house at Webster Creek I was sent to the local convent school situated on the edge of a town twenty-five miles away. Webster Creek itself was tiny, not quite a blink-and-you'll-miss-it type of place, but near enough. There were seventeen other houses on two main roads with a pub, a petrol station, a shop-cum-post-office, a church, and a railway station, as well as, of course, the Creek itself. The village had once been of some importance which is why the station was there, although in recent times only four trains a day would stop: one coming from Sydney, one going to Sydney; and again, one coming, one going, not necessarily to or from Sydney but in that general direction. It was very rare that a passenger would alight, normally just the post and the newspapers and perhaps a spare tractor part to be left in the care of the station-master.

In the 1850s the area had been known for gold-mine prospecting and Webster Creek had then been quite a sizeable town catering to those who camped the banks of the Creek panning for gold and those who had set up in the hills digging mine shafts. Eventually the belief in the possibility of gold had dried up although a couple of fortunes had been made in the interim. Those who stayed in the region settled small farms where they grew wheat and raised sheep and cattle. Others planted orchards and soon the area which had been known as a gold-rush region was renowned for its crops of golden delicious apples. When the gold-rush had failed, many of the Chinese who had been lackeys to the more prosperous prospectors and who had squatted on the Creek bank swishing water in a pan, eyes seeking the glint of a speck of gold amongst stones, stayed in the area with the result that the region had more than its fair share of Chinese restaurants. Looking back the area was incredibly multi-racial, although none of us thought of it like that at the time, we were all Aussies whose folks had just happened to come from a wide variety of places. There were the Italians and Greeks, as well as Christian immigrants fleeing from persecution in the Middle East: the Turks, the Syrians, the Lebanese, the Palestinians, the Coptic Egyptians. I went to school with all of them. There we all were in that one convent school, a

United Nations of girls being taught by Irish, Spanish, French and Italian nuns. First- and second-generation Australians with our religion binding us together.

The Creek itself, a tributary of the Macquarie River, wound its way between a number of sleepy rural villages, skirting the nearby mountains. I spent many hours exploring its banks, sometimes the Creek banks would come so close that I could jump across to the other side while at other places the banks would widen so far and the Creek become so deep that there would be islets in the centre where a tree or two would grow. I never swam to any of those islets. Secretly I was afraid of deep water and so would just sit on the bank and dangle my legs or wade in until I was knee deep, only to be overcome by an anxiety that would make me turn and wade back to the bank. Only where the water ran shallow over pebbles did I cross to the other bank and pass long hours watching the movements of the dragonflies. I never saw the Creek dry up not even after a year or two of drought – many times I saw it flooded, overflowing the banks I had played on, covering the fields, lapping at the side of the road, sometimes spilling over an inch or two so that when the car drove through, the water would hiss as it parted for the tyres. Normally I loved this, found the sound of running water exciting, loved the glassy sheen of fields covered in water. Sometimes, though, I was afraid.

One time in particular Mary and I were returning home after a visit to Sydney. At home it had been raining for a week, sheet upon sheet of rain. As we neared home we had to cross a bridge where the Creek joined the river. Usually there was a drop of twenty or so feet between river and bridge, but on this occasion the water lapped at the bridge, angrily hurling broken tree branches onto the road. Mary stopped the car and goggle-eyed we both stared at the tumult of water. I knew she was afraid, knew that she was thinking, what if we are in the middle of the bridge when the water decides at that very moment to pour over the top of the bridge and sweep the car – with us in it – away? Mary was not a coward, I think I can count on two, possibly three fingers the times I saw her afraid and that day at the bridge is one of them. Her fear was infectious and I leant forward from where I sat on the back seat and rested my chin on the front seat, eyes flicking from her face to the water. She swallowed and looking at me asked whether I thought we should turn around and detour the river to get home, a detour of a bit over one hundred miles, or make a dash over the bridge.

Mary was always asking what I thought, although she rarely, if ever, took my advice. In this instance I shrugged, thinking – if we make a dash for it and the car stalls in the middle and then won't start again, then we will have to get out into the rain and walk to the other side with all that water tumbling underneath our feet. What if at that very moment the water comes pouring over the side of the bridge. I thought we should make the detour.

I was glad that I had remained silent when Mary made the decision to drive across. She put the car into gear and sat revving the engine for a minute, then her leg shot forward to flatten the accelerator. We were over that bridge in a flash but Mary didn't remove her foot from the accelerator until we reached home when, after switching off the engine, she sat back against her seat and glanced my way. I who had kept my chin resting on top of the seat looking out through the windscreen suddenly started to cry. A loud, wailing 'I've-been-afraid' cry, and Mary turned and taking my face in her hands kissed my wet cheeks and nose and forehead and eyes, for she too had been afraid.

She was good like that was Mary, would never have dreamt of telling me to stop crying and behave like a big girl, for I cried rarely. I could fall and skin my knees and I wouldn't cry, I would just pick myself up and walk on. Yet, on the strangest, most unlikely occasions I would cry and have to be put to bed because I had made myself sick from crying. Mary would kiss me on the face as I lay in bed, eyes swollen red, head throbbing, stomach churning from the devastation of tears. It remains one of my favourite things, to have someone hold my face in their hands, to touch my face with their fingertips. It doesn't even have to be accompanied by a kiss. I go all wobbly, have thought myself in love quite simply because of that gesture. So few people do it, lift their hands to cup another's face, palm against cheek, eyes connecting.

Despite these periodic floods our house was never in danger, for the Creek flowed away from us to join the Macquarie, as did a number of other creeks in the region. It was those who lived further downstream who were often flooded out of their homes. The local roads when covered in an inch or so of creek water were never impassable, thus once I started going to school I never missed a day.

I loved school: the books, the schoolwork, the homework, the nuns. I was proud of my school uniform and liked sitting at my desk, chewing my pencil and writing neatly in my lined exercise books. Every morning Mary drove me to school and in the afternoon would come and collect me, at a variety of times, depending on whether I had netball practice. Once a week, on Saturday mornings, she would take me to the local library and we would choose four books each to take home and read. I kept a list of all the books that I read so that I would not make the mistake of getting the same book out again. It was not a big library but I had never seen so many books in my entire life and every time I approached the steps with Mary, and later on my own, I would feel dread at the thought of all those books and only being able to choose four. On the occasions that I was allowed to work on a school project in there, the librarian having helped me to choose books to look at, reference books that I wasn't allowed to take home, I wasted a good part of the time adrift in fantasies of what it would be like to live in the library, tucked away in the corner. I tried to devise a way to get locked in, and although I was often the last to leave, it was inevitable that leave I did. Sometimes I think fondly of those reading lists which I kept and wish I still had them so that on a spare day I could perhaps go to the library and look at some of the books I read in a particular year, and try to remember, try to see, the girl that I was, who would become me. For I firmly believe that I am little more than a composite of all the characters in books that I have ever read. A slow gleaning of impressions of how to be and that there is not really a me at all.

My aptitude for school took Mary by surprise, from the first day when she had walked me to the gate and stood waiting for me to turn and wave as I walked up the path. Many years later she told me how much it had hurt her that I hadn't turned to wave goodbye. Although we had spent every day together for the previous seven years I had just walked away from her on that first day of school. She told me later that she cried. Cried all the way home then kept herself frantically busy all day so as not to brood. I can't remember what I felt in my crisp school tunic, ankle socks and brown lace-up shoes so new that they squeaked with every footstep. I can't have realized what was happening. Mary had told me I was there for the day, so there for the day I was.

When she came to collect me at the end of that first day I was already in trouble and Sister Therese waited with me to have a word with Mary when she arrived. I waited in the car while they sat on a seat in the playground and Sister Therese informed Mary that I was a spoilt little girl who was too used to having her own way and this must be reined in, this must be brought to a stop. Mary nodded, slightly in awe of Sister Therese, needing to be careful, for she had fibbed on my application form and said that she was a widow, which was why Sister Therese called her Mrs McCloskey. Mary, fearing that I had been caught with my hand in another girl's school case, worked up the courage to ask what I had done wrong.

Sister Therese told Mary that when she had left the classroom for a moment, just for a moment she emphasized, she had asked all the girls to sit quietly and read their books until she returned. Upon her return she had found her classroom, her girls, in an uproar, and I standing on my desk singing and dancing, entertaining the class. When I had been gently rebuked for my naughtiness I had dared to answer back and Sister Therese had had to ask me to take my seat and sit in the corridor. After allowing a suitable time to pass for me to reflect on the unsuitability of my behaviour, Sister Therese had come out to have a little chat and bring me in to rejoin the class, only to find that I had taken myself out into the sun where I had removed my shoes and socks, to play in the grass. She had called me over. Look at you, Miss McCloskey, your feet are filthy, your tunic is grubby, and you've only been here for an hour. I looked at my feet and at my grass stained tunic and then back up at her, but when I did not respond she knelt in front of me, bringing herself to my level, and taking my arms shook me a little saying that I was bad, bad, bad and that Little Baby Jesus did not like bad little girls. So upset did she seem that I moved forward into her bosom from which I murmured don't be angry with me. It had always worked with Mary and so it did with Sister Therese: her arms wrapped around me and she stroked my hair, and I allowed myself to remain enveloped by the volumes of fabric that comprised her habit and her veil. She smelled of talc and I placed my arms around her neck, amply protected by her veil, as she lifted me and carried me into the washroom where she stood me in the sink to bath my feet and my legs before drying them with toilet tissue and then replacing my socks and shoes.

Still, it had been necessary for her to tell Mary about my poor behaviour. I had difficulty, it seemed, in doing as I was asked. Sister Therese added that she was trying to be understanding for she knew that I had never been to school and that it might take me a little while to settle in. At home Mary drummed into me that I must do what the nuns requested of me. She had been educated by the nuns and wanted the same for me. So, when Sister Therese said sit, I sat. When she said stand, I stood. I became the quietest, best-behaved girl in the class. I became Sister Therese's favourite, whenever we went on a day trip there I was holding her hand.

By the end of my first year I was top of the class. I seemed clever: I devoured books, I picked up words, ideas and lessons quickly. I steamed through my homework as soon as I arrived home, I would sit at the kitchen table in my school uniform and only when I had finished would I change my clothes and go out to play. It was a habit that remained for the duration of my school years. By the end of my first year I had become a prize pupil and as I accepted my prize from Sister Therese at the school assembly I swallowed back bitter tears of disappointment as I was handed a small framed picture of the Crucifixion. It was the ugliest picture I had ever seen: why on earth was Jesus yellow? I didn't understand. Jesus hadn't looked like that, Gauguin had got it wrong.

Understandably my popularity with the nuns did not endear me to my classmates. They feared me to some degree, feared my ability to misbehave in all manner of ways but still come out favourite with the nuns, whom we privately called the God squad. There were a couple of half-hearted attempts at friendship, but I found the other girls prissy and silly given, as they were, to playing mothers and babies. On the few occasions that I joined in I was allocated the role of father – he who went out to work, and would then come home, pat his baby on the head and kiss his wife on the cheek. This necessitated me, early on in the game, leaving the area that was designated as the house and going and sitting on the grass some way to the side, where initially I watched what went on in the 'house'. I rapidly found this tiresome and took to reading my book, then as the bell rang signalling the end of our lunch break I would be rapidly summoned back to the house to play my role of daddy returning home at the end of the day. From the sidelines, as I listened to the playful prattle of the game, I gradually came to be relieved that I was playing father. Absent from the cooing over baby. Dressing baby up. Feeding baby. Taking baby for a walk in the pram. Having friends for tea and comparing babies. I, as daddy, was well out of it, out of the house, at work, removed from it all, reading my book. Slowly I inched myself further and further away, until one day when I was summoned to return home to my wife and baby I had disappeared and was nowhere to be found. I was never asked to play again, was screamed at by my tearful 'wife' that I had completely, utterly and totally ruined the game.

I didn't mind my subsequent exclusion, and nor really did they, for they had found me slightly difficult to handle. I was not interested in their girly games but nor was I a tomboy. I was silent and enjoyed being on my own and when not reading sat gazing into space and thinking, inventing stories which eventually I would start to keep in a notebook. Mary worried about my friendless state, worried about her child who begged not to have to go to a birthday party, but never forced me to go. When I was happy she was happy, so she said. If I had wanted to make the appropriate overtures I know that I could have made friends, but somehow I couldn't be bothered.

It is, though, a strange thing how I can remember all the faces of those girls with whom I went to school. I can put names to individual faces. In my mind's eye I can see us all lined up in rows in the school photographs taken each year, girls that I was at school with for a little over a decade and then never saw again after we graduated. I have such a poor memory for names, can sit next to a person at a dinner and then the next time I meet them I am unable to remember their name. It embarrasses me. Yet I can remember the faces and names of all those girls. Memory is a strange thing, is it not?

Ella keeps me informed of the happenings at Webster Creek. Ella who, you ask? Would it be fair to call her my childhood rival? That is, perhaps, too strong a description. Later I shall tell of her.

When Ella told me of Sister Therese's death and that she had only been thirty-nine, I wept for the girl who, twenty years previously, had knelt in front of me and begged me to be good. I thought of how little I knew of her and yet how much I had loved her. I remembered how, running after her in the playground, I would beg her to come and skip with us and she would jump, holding her veil with one hand and lifting her long skirts with the other, as we turned the rope and chanted Sacred Heart, Sacred Heart, tell us the name of her sweetheart. Then rattling off the alphabet we would always stop at J, and how she would laugh while we shouted every boy's name beginning with J that we could possibly think of, all the while knowing that Sister Therese's sweetheart was Jesus.

It is somehow painful to think that I'll never know the colour of her hair, hidden away all those years under a veil. What had she looked like at night when she removed it? Did she sometimes see in the mirror a girl with another name, a name discarded in favour of Therese, a girl who had given up lipstick and boys, babies and marriage. Was she ever afraid, praying that her decision had not been a mistake? Or had she a sense of something greater, more complex than her own physicality? Or, simply, had she desired to live within a community of women? I never asked, so I'll never know.

Once when she went on pilgrimage to Lourdes I prayed for her, fearful that she might never return. France was forever from rural Australia. But she had, bringing with her a small phial of holy water which I kept on my bedside table, and dusted religiously each week.

Then ruthlessly, almost overnight, I stopped speaking to her. I was fifteen. She was always kind when our paths did cross, which was surprisingly little given the smallness of the school. At the time I thought that she hadn't noticed that I was brusque and short in conversation, but of course she had. How many times must that have happened to her, those young girls that she had nurtured turning away as teenagers, patronizing her, disdaining her, mocking her.

What, I like to imagine myself asking, had her goodness brought her? A short illness, a too-young death, a little grassy plot in the graveyard of the nunnery shaded by a cherry tree. Ella, who has become a nun herself, tells me that Sister Therese's tree has the biggest juiciest cherries of any of the trees in the graveyard, and that this is so even when there is a drought. Even then there is an abundance of brilliant red cherries to be had from her tree. At this point Ella always smiles in that sure, knowing way of hers, which somehow reminds me of Sister Therese, and says that she believes that this is a miracle, and I do not contradict her.

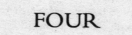

FOUR

Tedium: these women weary me. I pinch the bridge of my nose with my fingers, then rub my eyes thinking that truly I cannot be bothered to read any further. I slide the ledger onto the desk, from where it has been resting on my legs. An immense marbled tome containing a collection of ballads and broadsides that have been glued onto pages, all about women who have murdered their husbands. A plethora of women. What had begun with my hand hungrily turning page after page to discover yet another dead husband has turned into a litany of names, a surfeit, a glut, an engorgement of mariticidal women. With the result that I have lost interest as I catalogue each individual name:

i   *The Burnynge of Anne Bruen* (1592)
ii   *A True Discourse of the Practises of Elizabeth Caldwell* (1603)
iii   *The Arraygnement and Burnynge of Margaret Ferne – Seede for the Murther of her Late Husband* (1608)
iv   *The wooman [sic] that was Lately burnt in Sainte Georges fieldes for the murther of her Husband* (1608)
v   *A Warning for All Desperate Women By the Example of Alice Davis* (1628)
vi   *The Last Dying Speech and Confession of Alice Clarke, who was Executed* (1636)
vii   *Murther, Murther. Or, A Bloody Relation How Anne Hamton . . . By Poyson Murthered Her Husband . . . being Assisted and Counselled Thereunto by Margaret Harwood* (1641)
viii   *A Warning for Bad Wives: Or, The Manner of the Burnyng of Sarah Elston* (1678)

And so on and so forth.

I flick through the pages which have been hand numbered in the corner to the last page – 77 – and cannot bear the thought of cataloguing another sixty accounts of plotting, of poisoning, of heads staved in, of women swinging from the gallows. I am bored. It is too easy to imagine wishing to kill one's husband, to find one's partner monotonous, and thus highly dispensable.

Outside the sun is shining and I am sitting indoors with a ledger of pamphlets on women long dead. It is the first warm day of the year and I want to be outside feeling the sunshine on my face, breathing warm air, walking, feeling bones and joints beginning to unlock from the long English winter. I have opened the windows for the first time in six months and noises tumble through enticing me out. I telephone Edmund, the blue sky and sunshine must be shared. He answers on the fifth ring, delighted that I have called, I can hear the pleasure in his voice as he says my name. He thanks me for interrupting his lousy day in which he has managed to write eight lines in two and a half hours. Unsympathetically I laugh; if it is so awful why hasn't he called me to suggest a walk. He tells me that he is in 'self-punishment mode', that he is in the mood for working himself into a complete, utter and total state about how useless he is, and that since he seemed to be succeeding, he hadn't wanted to interrupt the flow. At least, he tells me, if I am good at getting myself into a state then I know that I am good at something, rather than nothing. I tell him to shut up and put a jacket on, I'll be there in a minute.

He sits on the brick wall waiting for me and we set off walking immediately. It is unspoken that we will walk across the Heath – we always do. We walk along, our stride matching, hardly talking. It is our way. Edmund is one of the few, if not the only person I like to walk with because of his silence. He attempts neither small talk nor a serious conversation. Now and then he draws my attention to the colour of some berries, or a bird, or a leaf wafting through the sky from who knows where, as most of the trees are still bare of leaves.

We smile at each other, slightly derisively, at the amount of flesh that is unearthing itself from the long winter. Flesh, worm-like white, too revolting for description. Despite the sunshine the day is not warm but there are bare arms and legs. Joggers virtually unclothed. The English, I say, are fucking weird. No sense, no feeling, Edmund responds. I say that the winters seem to be getting longer the longer that I'm in England, and he agrees, either that or we are getting old. In Waterlow Park we find a seat to rest on and enjoy the sunshine but it is too cold to remain still so we resume walking, down past Highgate cemetery and back onto the Heath. As we pass the cemetery I stretch an arm through the railing, delighted at the sight of a swath of lily of the valley, picking as many as are within arm's reach. This is a walk I have done many times with Edmund, and only with him do I come here. It would be a strange thing to come here on my own and the thought crosses my mind that when he is dead I shall either never come here again or have to come here on my own. The possibility that I might miss Edmund when he is dead is a curious one and not one I wish to examine.

I glance at his face and catching my look he smiles. I say that I do enjoy walking with him and I can tell that this has pleased him by the flourish with which he opens his gate and steps aside to allow me to pass through first. I have always loved his flat – the ground floor of a Victorian house with large light-filled rooms. They are rooms in which I am immediately comfortable, with their dark, heavy furniture, piles of books, vases of flowers and his own watercolours framed on the walls. The first time I visited I thought that the flowers might be to impress me, but they were not, it is his one extravagance, fresh flowers in every room. He cannot walk past a flower stall without stopping to look, touching petals and leaves, burying his face in bunch after bunch. When he buys flowers it can take him hours, and he will not be rushed. The act of choosing is a ceremony within itself, a meditation. Today his rooms are full of daffodils, from almost-white jonquils to the gaudiest yellow nozzle, thrusting rudely out.

It is a restful flat, gentle but solid, chintz sofas, ticking clock, highly waxed floor with rugs, an open fire which is not just for decoration. You know the type of room I mean, that the English of a certain class seem to inhabit. All that is missing are the dogs by the fire. But Edmund loathes dogs, so that is that. His garden, considering his love of flowers, is a simple expanse of green with a birdbath and trellises on all sides for roses, taken from cuttings from Hermione's house in Suffolk. The first time I came to the house the roses were in bloom and their smell had climbed the steps onto his terrace and wandered in through the glass doors to intoxicate us as we sat. I was enchanted. It is a feeling that has never passed. Away from the bookshop this is the only other place that I feel truly at home. Here, I am not a stranger, I feel less inhibited.

In the garden we eat our lunch, lightly buttered brown bread with smoked salmon. Edmund insists upon opening a bottle of white wine – very dry, very chilled, to celebrate the sunshine. We eat in a comfortable silence, but I am aware by the way he gulps his wine that he is not happy. When I ask him if his discontent is due to his writing he laughs and says of course not, he is a bloody awful writer and he knows it and is used to it. He knows

93

that if he were not a Maskelyne no one would be interested in publishing his work.

No, he says rather tiredly, it is his gut that is depressing him. It has been over a month now that his gut has been troubling him, on and off. The pain will suddenly arrive, out of the blue, a gnawing sensation at his innards that will double him up and make him sweat and shake. I watch his fingers tremble slightly as they reach for his glass of wine which he drains in a mouthful, then refills. I ask him what the doctor says and he replies not a lot, that he has been given a prescription for drugs and if they don't work he is to go back. I ask him if there is blood when he goes to the toilet and he says not, but that he is either constipated or shit is running out of him in bucketloads. Then he apologizes because we are still eating. As he looks at me, swigging from his glass, I recall that years ago, out of the blue, he had said that I was crude. His statement had been posed as a question. But you are crude, Miss, aren't you? I was sitting at a dinner table surrounded by his friends, who were involved in conversations of their own, and I felt as if I had been kicked in the chest. My manners were no different from theirs. I had felt my eyes fill but fought the urge to weep and had blinked hard at my wine glass, then looked at Edmund, raised my eyebrow and agreed that yes, I was crude.

Was that what he was thinking now? That because I was an Australian I was vulgar? That because I had been born in the bush I was coarse? Leaning forward to refill his glass he said that I was the only person that he could speak with like this. Edmund proceeded to tell me how miserable he was in London at the moment, how he wanted to be in the country walking and painting his watercolours, a long way away from masses of people and the grime of the city. He was thinking of going away for a week or so. Did I fancy coming?

His question didn't surprise me. We had travelled together on many occasions. He was a pleasant travelling companion, not needy, nor ebullient, but a quiet presence at my side. Travelling with Edmund was almost like travelling on my own. But I couldn't possibly go away at the moment, I couldn't afford to close the shop for a couple of weeks. It was impossible. He looked petulant, muttering that I could if I really wanted to. He looked so dejected that I partially capitulated and agreed to a long weekend, four days, but no more than that.

His elation was palpable as he listed places we might possibly visit. He suddenly seemed like the old Edmund: excited, foot bouncing with nervous energy. I went into the kitchen to make some tea and he followed me, and as he leant against the bench with his hands in his pockets I suddenly desired him, could feel the heat gathering around my hips and spreading downwards.

We agreed to drive somewhere into the countryside, we would decide where exactly later. Edmund would get out his guidebooks and try to find an area that we hadn't visited together, somewhere I hadn't been to before.

As I watched him speak, I thought that it wasn't too late not to poison him. That there was no rule that said that I had to follow through with Edmund's murder. That I could stop now and no one would ever know what had happened. Edmund's stomach would eventually right itself and he would be well again. I couldn't imagine not having Edmund as my friend and that out of all the people I knew in London the person I was closest to was Edmund, and I could not imagine my life with him not in it.

As I left he walked me to the car, after carefully wrapping the stems of my bunch of lily of the valley in wet newspaper to keep them fresh. As we stood by the car chatting a dog bounded up, panting ingratiatingly, tongue lolling out of its mouth, and just as Edmund growled at it to fuck off, which it translated into an invitation to play, barking delightedly in response, just as I thought he might be going to kick it, a voice called that they were awfully sorry, Ibby heel. The body that belonged with the voice stopped beside the dog and as we both looked from the dog to its owner, Edmund's expression changed from you-should-keep-it-on-a-fucking-lead to one of polite sociability, and his mouth opened and closed without saying a word.

I watch him watching her – a typical North London girl – brown shiny hair, brown eyes, jeans, shirt, simple gold jewellery. As she bent to put Ibby on her lead he watched her breasts and the fall of her shirt where it opened to reveal her tawny skin. And in one very smooth downwards-upwards move his glance encompassed her waist, her crotch, her legs and then returned to her face. They smiled at each other as she apologized again and my eyes followed his as he watched her walk away. Then turning back to me still smiling he leans down and kisses me goodbye on the cheek, or more specifically on the corner of my mouth. We only shake hands when meeting at the bookshop, as Edmund prefers to maintain that formality when I am working. It is not a lingering kiss but in that split second I can smell on his breath the odour that indicates his arousal, betrays his lust. I am aware that it is Ibby's mistress and not I who is the object of his desire.

As I drive off I watch him in the rear-view mirror and imagine him going back inside and masturbating to his fantasies of her. For truly that is what Edmund is — a wanker. But what then does that mean I am, for momentarily doubting my plan? A fool? A simpleton?

ii

I remove the lily of the valley from the jug in which they sit and transfer the water that remains in the bottom of the jug to a bowl. I refill the jug, replace the flowers and return them to my bedside table where they have delighted me since I arrived home with them. Consulting my notebook I ascertain that just a couple of drops of the water in which the lilies have been kept will be enough to upset Edmund's constitution. Two drops. I fill the eyedropper and leave it ready by his cup and saucer, the ones with the lily of the valley pattern that I found in an antique market down the road.

He arrives punctually at four while I am rearranging my book display in the window. I am tense and irritable. We drink our tea in silence, he easily reads my mood and as he replaces his cup on the tray he stands to say that he thinks he will be off. I do not encourage him to stay but I wonder how far he will get before those two drops of lily of the valley water effect him. My notes say immediately after ingestion. Perhaps the dose has been too negligible?

I stare at his back as he stands at the kerb looking down the road. He stands with shoulders hunched, very still. It seems as if he has been standing there for an unimaginable amount of time, but a glance at my watch shows that it is not quite five minutes since his departure. Suddenly he turns and stares at me through the window, brow furrowed, then he returns his gaze to the kerb,

97

looking down, head turning to look to his left, then along to his right. He just stands there looking, turning his head, left to right. He might possibly stand there for ever, his posture implies. I can't possibly let him stand there like that, he is making an arse of himself. At the doorway I call him twice before he responds, shouting what without turning around to face me. In three strides I am at his side asking him to come inside and have another cup of tea. He shakes his head rapidly to tell me no, his gaze remaining fixed on the road. As I move to take a step down from the kerb into the road to force him to look at me he grabs my arm and wrenches me back. Wide-eyed, his dilated pupils bore into me. His spittle hits my face as, maintaining his clenched grip of my arm, his voice flatly states that I will drown. I blink rapidly a number of times, can't quite get my eyebrow to rise to its usual level of disdain. Where has all that water come from? Is he asking me or speaking to himself? What does one do when another is hallucinating? Hell. Should I play the game? I become aware that Janson, who sells music books next door, has moved to his window, all the better to see what is happening. We share a mutual lack of admiration Janson and I, and as I raise two fingers to him he chuckles and nods in mock civility but remains rooted at his window, watching. Turning to Edmund I say that the water seems very shallow and he surveys the road with a look of horror. Shallow, he says, shallow? No, it goes down for ever you know, there is no bottom. I say there must be because otherwise the footpath would be submerged. Edmund looks at me as if I am a complete cretin. No. No. No. The footpath is only a boundary, we are floating on the water. There is nothing underneath us but water, so we must be careful otherwise the water will lap over the edge of the footpath and seep into the bookshop and it will capsize and we will be submerged. He is very calm, his voice matter of fact. He crouches down and touches the road as if he were dipping his fingers into water. Standing up he looks at his fingertips and tells me that the water is very cold.

I take his hand which is clammy and ask him to come inside with me. When I add that we can monitor the water from the window he acquiesces. He sits in my window, in the chair that I have positioned him in, watching the road, turning every fifteen minutes or so to announce that the water is much too high, then returning to his vigil. I sit behind my desk unsure whether to close the shop or to proceed as usual, but the customers who do wander in hardly seem to notice Edmund. The few that do just gently smile at him as if perhaps he is my slightly retarded brother. After two very long hours have passed I finally hang the closed sign on the door. Edmund has dropped off to sleep and the street light accentuates an unbecoming rash spreading along his left cheekbone. I leave him as he is and proceed to count my day's takings.

One of the joys of selling books is that a majority of my income is in cash which allows me the delight of fiddling and diddling my accounts endlessly. As I work here alone and own the building my overheads are minimal, my actual running costs — aside from the purchase of books — are negligible. On an average day I take about four hundred pounds, on an exceptional day a couple of thousand, depending of course on the rarity of the books that I manage to sell. What I take through the shop I consider a bonus and only declare a third of it to the taxman. I think this is fair, all my mail order income is declared, it has to be as all the payments are by cheque or credit card. These days people enjoy buying books from home, from catalogues or from a website. It is not a consumer trend that I understand, for what is more enjoyable than to stand in a bookshop, eyes flicking from title to title to alight now and again on words that beckon, words that reach out and seduce so that one's hand lifts to touch, to take, to pull towards oneself. How many hours becoming days becoming years is it that I have meandered the rows of bookshelves? How many more in the future? I can't imagine a life without books: touching them, buying them, reading them. I nearly said writing them, but I'm not a writer, am I? Sometimes I forget.

Edmund stirs, blinking drowsy eyes in my direction. He is apologetic. I ask him what happened, although of course I know, and he tells me that he has no idea. Has it ever happened before? He answers no, but sounds aghast, appalled at the supposition that he might be prone to hallucinations. Is he thinking that perhaps he is just like his mother after all? That maybe this afternoon is a presentiment of things to come? He carries his seat over to where I am and disappears upstairs to return with whisky and two glasses. As he sips he picks up the book that I have been cataloguing and flicks through it.

Bloody hell – he pulls a face – what on earth is this? He directs a glance my way before turning to the title page: *A Narrative of the barbarous and Unheard of Murder of Mr John Hayes in 1726*, he reads aloud. Bloody hell, he repeats.

The first illustration, I tell him, shows John Hayes' wife Catherine assisting her two accomplices in decapitating him. Following his murder. Catherine, I say, is holding a tub for the blood to drip into while one of the men holds

Hayes' body steady as the other hacks away at his neck. Catherine's accomplices were Thomas Billings, a tailor, and Thomas Wood, a supposed friend of Hayes, both of whom had been lodging with the Hayes in London. Some accounts specify Wood as Catherine's lover, however, the reality was worse, for he was in fact her illegitimate son. Do I mean incest, Edmund asks? Yes, I say. He seems curious to know more, so I continue the story.

Catherine had plotted her husband's death and had the two men carry it out. The plan was that they would make him a wager that he could not drink six pints of wine without becoming intoxicated; a wager which he accepted. After drinking the required six pints Hayes had, unsurprisingly, collapsed on his bed in a drunken stupor. At this point Billings and Wood had entered the bedroom whereupon Billings hit Hayes on the head with a hatchet. The blow fractured his skull and made Hayes in his agony stamp on the floor. Wood, fearing the consequence of the noise, repeated the blow to his head many more times. During the murder Catherine had waited in the kitchen, but afterwards she entered the bedroom and suggested that they decapitate Hayes in order to make identification of the body difficult. They then severed the head from the body with a pocket knife, a somewhat laborious task, and when the bleeding had finally stopped Catherine had poured the blood down a wooden sink and they had proceeded to dismember the remainder of the body.

After this, the trio discussed what was to be done next. Catherine was for boiling the head in a pot until nothing but the skull remained which would prevent anyone from being able to identify John Hayes at all, but the two men agreed that the best way to rid themselves of the head was by throwing it into the Thames. Unfortunately for them a nightwatchman witnessed their action. Even more unfortunate was a not insignificant detail that they had overlooked: low tide. Thus when the head landed it was not with a splash but a splat as it came to rest in a mud bank.

The authorities, informed by the nightwatchman, retrieved the head and had it cleaned. The face was washed free of mud and blood and the hair combed, for the purpose of putting the head on public view the better to attempt an identification. The spot chosen was St Margaret's churchyard, Westminster, where the head was stuck on a pole.

Edmund holds the illustration depicting this scene very close to his face, studying it in detail. What, he wishes to know, happened to the rest of John Hayes' body? Thrown into a pond in what at the time was Marylebone Fields, I tell him. No one, however, could identify the head and a week after its discovery the parish officers, considering that the head might putrify if left in the open air, had it preserved in spirits in a glass jar.

Catherine meanwhile had set up house with Billings and Wood, and had employed herself in obtaining as much of her husband's estate as possible by sending fictitious letters in his name. It had been her offer to split her husband's estate three ways that had apparently convinced the two men to assist her.

John Hayes' friends soon become suspicious at his disappearance. Having independently viewed the decapitated head and seen similarities to their missing friend three of them visited Catherine separately, all being told differing stories as to his whereabouts. After comparing Catherine's explanations they decided to go to the police, with the result that Catherine, Billings and Wood were immediately arrested.

Coolly, Catherine requested to see the head, and when shown it threw herself on her knees crying out that, indeed, it was her dear husband's head. Embracing the glass jar in which it was kept she kissed the outside of it several times. The justice observing her actions was not impressed, however, and told her that if it was her husband's head she should view it more plainly, and that he would take it out of the glass jar for her, which he did, holding it up by the hair. Catherine, taking the head into her arms kissed it, begging to have a lock of the hair. When the justice replied that she had had too much of him already, Catherine fainted.

Imagine, I say to Edmund, taking a head in your arms, wet and reeking of spirits. A head that has had a number of hatchet blows to the skull and gaping wounds. A head with ragged pieces of skin around the neck from being mangled when cut off. A head in the early stages of decomposition from being in the open air for a week. Imagine kissing that head upon the lips.

Although Catherine continued to insist on her innocence, Wood rapidly followed Billings in making a full confession. At her trial Catherine pleaded not guilty, only relenting after being found guilty, but still declaring herself innocent because the crime had not actually been committed by her own two hands. Sentenced to burn at the stake, she was drawn upon a sledge to the place of execution, where she was bound with an iron chain which ran around her waist and under her arms. Around her neck a rope was placed not only for restraint but for the purpose of allowing the executioner the merciful action of breaking her neck just as the fire was started. Inopportunely for Catherine the faggots had been mixed with a great quantity of light brushwood and straw with the result that the fire immediately blazed upwards causing the executioner to drop the rope. Thus, Catherine was burned alive.

Reduced to ash in four hours. Which is what, I say to Edmund, you can see in the third illustration: a woman burning to death, the stench of her own burning flesh filling her nostrils.

Mary and Lucille met one Saturday morning when Mary and I were walking through Jekyll's department store, for although we were not Jekyll's customers we used their car park at the back of the store to leave the car while we shopped elsewhere. We had stopped to look at the scarves on that spring morning – Mary had said that it seemed a spring kind of thing to do – to stand and finger that glorious tumble of fabrics in every colour and combination of colour imaginable.

Then there she was at our side – Lucille, her name tag said – in the crisp Jekyll uniform. With her shiny strawberry blonde hair that swung at the sides of her well-made-up face, her long white fingers with long bright pink painted nails, she appeared to be everything that Mary was not. She looked at Mary and smiled, a fake salesperson type of smile, her mouth opening to show two neat rows of white teeth between lips whose colour matched her fingernails. Lucille's claim to fame was that she knew how to tie a scarf one hundred and one different ways, and her boss at Jekyll's had printed a small leaflet that detailed step-by-step diagrams, hand drawn by Lucille, on how to tie a scarf in twenty of the one hundred and one ways that only she knew. The leaflet came free with a scarf, or could be purchased for twenty-five cents.

My hackles rose and instinctively, protectively, I moved closer to Mary, hooking my arm through hers. My Mary in her jeans and shirt, cropped curls and no make-up, her rough calloused hands catching on the delicate fabrics of the scarves. Hands that had spent the past five years coaxing fruit and vegetables into growth, which she then sold on a stall at the front of the house underneath a big gum tree. It was only this year that she had begun to prosper enough to be able to employ two local boys to help her with the harder work.

Thrusting my chin in the air I told Lucille that we were just looking as she enquired if we needed assistance. She smiled at me, a smile that told me that she knew that we were poor, that we were not going to buy anything, that the only way that Mary and I would have a scarf from Jekyll's was if we stole one. I wanted to shout that neither Mary nor I stole any more, not since we had moved to Webster Creek, but of course I did not.

She moved off to the side folding and rearranging squares of fabric, neatly laying them out according to colour. My arm that was slotted into Mary's tried to edge her away, but she stood there determinedly, lifting scarf after scarf, shaking them open to look at, then refolding and replacing them on the table. When I persisted in trying to pull her away she shook off my hand with irritation and moved to Lucille's side. I deliberately stood apart while Mary and Lucille discussed the colour that would most suit Mary. In the end Mary purchased nothing, but just as we were walking away Lucille followed and touching Mary on the arm gave her one of her scarf-tying leaflets for free. Mary offered to pay, but Lucille insisted that the leaflet was free.

Four months were to pass before Mary told me one evening as she tucked me into bed, that she had been having morning coffee with Lucille after dropping me off at school. Although I was twelve it was still our ritual for Mary to tuck me in, kiss me on the eyes and then switch out the light. She had told me after kisses, her face hovering over mine, one hand holding the sheet and blankets near my chin, told me that she had invited Lucille and her daughter to our house, for supper. Lucille who? I had asked. Lucille from Jekyll's, Mary had replied.

I was furious, unbelievably so. I sulked; I slammed doors; I gave Mary the silent treatment. But all to no avail. Lucille and her daughter had been invited for supper and that was that. I found it impossible to believe that Mary was serious. Mary did not have friends. She and I were alike in that way. Mary and I didn't need friends, for we had each other. We told each other everything, or so I had thought, for she had not told me of her blossoming friendship with Lucille. When they arrived I hardly said a word throughout the meal unless it was unavoidable. Lucille's daughter was a miniature version of her mother, pretty and doll-like. I recognized Ella from school, I had seen her in the playground, she was a year younger than me. They terrified me, Lucille and Ella. They were like people in television programmes: pretty, clean, neat. I had no idea what to say to them but Mary chattered gaily talking about books and fruit and vegetables.

In the days that followed I expected Mary to apologize, to say that actually it had all been a big mistake, but she didn't. Nor did she ask me why I was quiet, or grumpy, or sulking. She seemed to ignore me, lost in making plans to see Lucille, devising an outing as a foursome. The Saturday excursions became a regular feature and before long were spilling over into Sundays. We swam, went on picnics and explored the countryside. We went to the movies and sat in the ice-cream parlour sharing a variety of flavours. Gradually I came around, by which I mean that although I refused to accept Lucille and Ella as permanent features of our life, I stopped ignoring them and deigned to join in the fun, even enjoying myself on occasion, but only now and then.

Who, what, when, where, or why the decision was made that Lucille and Ella should share our house I will never know, I was not consulted, merely informed after the event. Mary told me casually, over supper one evening. Ella could have the spare room and Lucille would share Mary's room. I wanted to shout no. Wanted to throw myself on the floor and flail my arms and my legs and cry no, no, no. But I didn't. I sat paralysed, with my fork halfway between my plate and mouth, precariously balancing peas, feeling my heartbeat vibrate throughout my body. Swallowing hard I managed to get the peas into my mouth, where they were chewed over and over before my throat would open to allow the green mush to slide down.

Mary, not noticing my lack of response, continued talking. As I watched her speak my temples throbbed. Somehow, somewhere, I had lost my footing, lost my grip. She was no longer mine, had not been mine for some months now following the beginning of her relationship with Lucille. She no longer confided in me, I no longer confided in her, although I made a pretence of doing so, providing the minimum details of what my day at school had been like. I felt as if I was sitting opposite someone I didn't know. This woman was not my mother. Why had she changed? Why, I wanted to scream at her, why do you want this other person, why am I no longer enough for you, why don't you love me any more? Instead I sat and finished my peas, trying to look unperturbed.

So five years after Mary and I had moved into Webster Creek, Lucille and Ella joined us, accompanied by a great many boxes of clothes and pieces of furniture so that Mary's and my house was no longer recognizable as ours. In the evenings Lucille would sew and soon everything that could be covered was, in the most bright patterned fabrics imaginable – cushions, tables, beds, windows – before she turned her attention to Mary and my wardrobe, making skirts and blouses and dresses, all run up on her Singer sewing machine. At Jekyll's she was now only working part time and so took over the household chores. Her presence was palpable, right down to the contents of my lunch box, which no longer merely contained a Vegemite sandwich. Mary thought Lucille was perfect, she said so. The way Lucille would read women's magazines and cut out the recipes which she would glue in three different scrapbooks depending on whether it was a starter, a main course or pudding. How she would knit cardigans and sweaters that always looked as good as the one the model wore on the cover of the knitting pattern. How despite all her knitting and sewing and cooking Lucille still had energy to spare and turned her hand to making preserves and pies from the fruit and vegetables that had not been sold on Mary's stall, which were such a success that in order to keep up with the demand Mary rented an additional field. And Mary herself smiled more often and looked a lot less tired than the days before Lucille and Ella had moved in.

In the years that followed I felt like a visitor in my own home. Yes, I ate the food that Lucille cooked, wore the clothes that she made, but I felt less and less a part of the foursome. I felt like a ghost. I caught the bus into town to school as did Ella, who would sit at the back chatting with her friends while I would sit at the front reading a book. She and I were neither friends nor enemies, we had little in common, yet I saw her as my rival. Her bedroom was crammed with dolls in all manner of period costumes from Elizabethan to Barbie. She had suitcases filled with dolls' clothes that she would spend hours changing them into, many made by Lucille from fabric remnants. She would sit in front of the television combing her dolls' hair, whispering in their ears about the programme that we were watching. My bedroom was exactly the opposite, filled with books, the most garish object a quilt that Lucille had made for me on their first Christmas in residence. Aside from a brush and comb on my dressing-table the room was bereft of clutter. I sat at my dressing-table to write, there was no space for a desk. There I wrote my diary, turgid pages full of longing and nostalgia for the days prior to Lucille and Ella. Days of order. Days of stillness. Days of silence.

Sometimes I would sit on my bed and through the window watch Mary in the field tending her vegetables. Quite literally my heart would ache, my chest tighten, as I watched her, and I would imagine being able to run out to where she was and throw my arms around her and tell her that I loved her. But I never did. I would watch the three of them laughing in the garden, and I knew that all it would take was for me to get off my bed and go out and join them. But I could not.

Did Mary worry about me? Did she privately discuss her concern with Lucille about what on earth was to be done with me? Possibly so, but she believed it best to just leave me alone, that I would come around. For I wasn't miserable all the time. When I forgot to wallow in my misery I had as much fun as the others on the adventures that Lucille invented for us. Oh yes, I would be a liar to say that I was miserable all the time. No one can be as unhappy as I seem to remember being, not all the time, otherwise they would just curl up and die.

In my naïvety it never occurred to me that Mary and Lucille might be more than best friends, although I saw them kiss and hug each other and knew that they shared a double bed. They were two women who loved each other but a more intimate, physical side to their relationship was one that had not occurred to me. One afternoon, in which Ella had gone off to a girlfriend's house, I overheard Lucille laughing very loudly in their bedroom. Her laugh was raucous and I wanted to know what was going on, what was so hilariously funny, so I walked from my bedroom through the kitchen but before I reached the bedroom door I could see them both reflected in their bedroom mirror. Lucille was not laughing but weeping, her face distorted, her body shaking as if in pain, Mary was holding her by the upper arms and attempting to quieten her. I watched Mary reflected in the mirror slowly soothe Lucille, stroke her back through the fabric of her dress, caress her hair, kiss her on the lips. Not the type of kisses that I received from her but long, hard, pressing kisses, the forcing-open-of-lips kisses. I watched, unable, unwilling to stop watching, as Mary's hand slid up Lucille's bare leg and under her dress as they continued to kiss. I didn't even avert my gaze as they undressed and lay on the bed, I merely moved very quietly so that I could see them better reflected in the mirror and held my breath for as long as I possibly could so that they wouldn't hear my breathing. I watched for some time before sneaking into my bedroom and lay on my bed, chest jerking with the pounding of my heart. Through my bedroom wall which was also their bedroom wall I could hear their noises, and I strained to decipher their words to each other.

In the days and weeks that followed my eyes lingered over them, Mary and Lucille, on their hands, their legs, their mouths. I noticed all the gestures that passed between them, all those everyday occurrences which suddenly assumed significance. Repeatedly my mind replayed what I had seen. Over and over. At night I would press my ear to the wall desperately straining to hear the sounds of their lovemaking. I watched the other girls at school and tried to imagine engaging in a similar activity with them. Girls, however, did not interest me, but then neither did boys. When I undressed I looked at myself in the mirror with avid interest. I was fifteen and a late developer, my breasts had only just begun to swell, hard lumps that were painful under my fingertips. Lying on my bed, I opened my legs to look at myself in my hand mirror which I held in a variety of positions. I opened myself with my fingers, exploring, but felt nothing, neither a sensation of pleasure nor displeasure, just moist flesh. Then I would hold my fingers to my nose sniffing the slightly pungent smell which I did not dislike. Beyond my own explorations, I had no desire to touch nor be touched. When Ella attempted to tell me of her experiences with her boyfriends I discouraged her with a brusque disinterest and soon she stopped trying to share her exploits with me. I was still a virgin on my eighteenth birthday and saw no reason to change the status quo. The men that I desired were those whom I encountered between the pages of books.

What would have become of me if Mary hadn't died is one of those impossible, unanswerable questions that periodically reverberate through my mind. For without her death I would have remained in Webster Creek and never have moved to London. I was not adventurous, not in the least, could not imagine a life away from Mary, for if she had not died I would never have left her. Although I knew that I wished to write, I planned to go no further afield than the local college to study English. Mary's death, on a very hot still afternoon three weeks after my eighteenth birthday, changed all that. Certainly I wouldn't be sitting here in the bookshop, and any alternative life, one outside the bookshop, is unfathomable.

On that hot afternoon Mary and I were alone in the house. It is a strange thing how all my memories seem to be of hot afternoons, they can't all be, of course, only in my memory are they so. On this particular afternoon Lucille was delivering her preserves to a small shop in town that had begun to stock them and Ella was out with her most recent boyfriend. When Mary had slipped while walking up the back steps I had laughed as I had asked her if she was all right, and she had laughed embarrassedly that she was, as her hand had moved to touch her brow which she had hit against the concrete step. Her forehead swelled rapidly and after ten minutes she had decided that she would have a lie down. Her head didn't hurt but she felt a little shaky and breathless. With ice cubes wrapped in a tea towel to press against her head she retreated to her bedroom.

I sat at the kitchen table sorting baskets of strawberries we had picked, relishing the silence, pleased that Lucille and Ella were absent. When I had finished I walked along to Mary's room but could see from her reflection in the mirror that she was sleeping and so I left her to rest. As one hour became two I grew annoyed, for she never slept this long, I was irritated that she was wasting our afternoon together in sleep. I strode in, mouth set, determined to waken her. She looked peaceful, her hands tucked under one cheek.

It was a curious thing standing there, looking at her, at the purple black bruise on her swollen brow. In my gut I knew that she was not alive, even though her face was the same; aside from the bruise she looked no different. I stood in the stillness watching her and when the rose bush at her open window rustled in the most vague of breezes I started in a guilty way and felt fear rushing through my bowels. I grabbed my trembling lip between my teeth and considered reaching out my hand to shake her shoulder but was unable to do so. My mind formulated her name but my voice would not cooperate. I tried to whisper M, but nothing happened with my lips. M: Mary, mother, mummy, mum. The M-word. She couldn't be dead. I stood over her and closed my eyes and willed her to open hers when I opened mine after a slow, very slow count of ten. But she did not. Would not. Could not. Never would.

I left her side to call an ambulance, thinking as I spoke into the receiver that we would all have a good laugh about this later, about how Miss had had a panic attack and called an ambulance. I nearly laughed in relief down the telephone as I imagined our later laughter. The ambulance arrived, then the police, then Lucille and Ella with her boyfriend, all within fifteen minutes of each other. I answered questions as politely as I could, while Lucille was sedated and put to bed in my room. She wept for four days, confined to bed, unable to eat, she just lay there, weeping. During the day I organized the funeral and in the evening I slept in Mary's bed. The bed she had lain on and died on. Mary and Lucille's bed. The bed in which Mary and I had slept together when we first moved to Webster Creek. Throughout the preparations for her funeral I slept a deep dreamless sleep and awoke every morning refreshed and ready for the day.

The funeral itself was large, I had no idea that Mary had come to know so many people. All the regulars who visited her stall were there, friends of hers and Lucille, my nuns from school, Ella's friends. After the service Mary was cremated and we then buried her ashes in the garden, near the rose bush under her bedroom window. Lucille still lives there, says that she can't imagine leaving. She still has the stall selling fruit and vegetables. In the wardrobe all Mary's clothes still hang, her perfume is on the dressing-table, the book she was reading when she died is still on the bedside table.

When I think of Mary's death it comes to me like a half-remembered dream, almost as if it had not happened at all and that it is something I invented, or thought I read in a book but have never been able to find the particular page again with those words written upon it. I didn't cry after her death, I felt that she was still with me, that she remains with me still, that I am a part of her and as long as I am alive so is she. Sometimes I think I see her in the distance, but that is just wishful thinking, as Mary herself would say. It seems madness to think that it is fifteen years since her death, for it seems like such a short time ago that I saw her, not fifteen years. Occasionally I wonder what we would talk about if she suddenly walked into the bookshop. What would she think of the adult that I have become? Would she like me? Would she like the bookshop?

Then, from time to time, a part of my mind clears, as if a dusty mirror were wiped clean showing me that truly I am never going to see Mary again, nor speak to her, and the enormity of her dead-ness, the absolute-ness of her lack of life, overwhelms me. Then I fear the chasm that opens wide in my skull, fight it by jumping to my feet, to do something, anything, so long as I am in motion. Then I think if only I had reached out to touch her shoulder, or said her name, she would have awoken. But I did not. I let her remain asleep. I let her go to wherever she is that is not here.

Reluctantly the chasm in my skull will close, the edges draw together and I am safe again, I can grow still and bear the silence. Then I allow myself to picture her, clearly, as if she were walking towards me, curls bouncing, hips swinging, clad in blue jeans. My Mary, I have no need of photographs to see her. I know that one day I will walk into a room and there she will be, as if all along that is where she has been, waiting for me. We'll look at each other, Mary and I, and she will say so there you are and it will be like we were never apart. I know it. I do.

FIVE

Be careful, it's poisonous, Edmund says, as he notices my fingers hooking under the bark of the yew tree attempting to lift a piece free. I start nervously, what, a small piece like this? He shrugs, unsure. Is it just the bark that is poisonous, I ask, already aware of the answer, but testing his response. He tells me that the bark, the needles and the seeds of the yew contain the poison taxine and having ingested taxine, my death, if I were lucky, would be sudden. Shock, then coma, followed by death due to cardiac arrest. If, however, I were unlucky I would suffer nausea, vomiting, diarrhoea, hallucinations, abdominal pain . . . He stops, and smiles, perhaps someone is poisoning me with yew, then he laughs, unlikely though for survival after poisoning is rare. I study the shape of his hand against the bark of the yew, blue veins, prominent under white skin, threading from his wrist to disappear in his long fingers. I place my hand beside his, stretching my fingers in a similar fashion, a smaller hand, more slight in bone structure. I lift my little finger to place it over his while I press my palm down so that the bark jabs into the soft flesh.

He moves away to look up through the limbs held aloft by supporting poles, and along their spreading branches, then walks the perimeter of the trunk, heel to toe, counting the feet as he walks. At the count of forty-seven he is once again at my side. More than two thousand years old, he tells me, my life thirty times over. I look at the former parish church, now redundant, by which the tree stands. A church perhaps built on this site because the yew already grew here and the site was seen as sacred, a church now stripped of its furnishings, locked against vandals.

Edmund walks towards the church, his contented humming drifting to me from over his receding shoulder. And as I watch him lay a blanket for our lunch, in a sun-trap corner tucked into the side of the church, I murmur to myself, but I shall lay a garland on your hearse, Edmund, of the dismal yew.

We eat our simple meal in silence — bread, cheese, olives, water — backs leaning against sun-warmed walls to gaze out at headstones and away over fields which seem in perpetual motion as sunlight duels with scudding clouds. My fingers pluck at the slightly damp stems of grass with which I am making a tidy pile on the blanket. Today is our last day on the island. This afternoon we shall take the ferry back to Portsmouth before a slow drive back to London on the minor roads. We are both rested, there is colour in our cheeks. We have climbed the two hundred steps down to Luccombe Chine to sit on the rocks, huddled over a fire built from driftwood to allay the bitter wind blowing in from the sea, warming our insides on whisky from the hipflasks that we carry, until we no longer feel the cold, playing guessing games as to where exactly it was that the dinosaur bones were found back in 1940-something. Laughing, as we had laboured on the upward climb, hands pressed against thighs to get some thrust, at how the benefits of the whisky had worn away by the time we reached the top. Our four days had been frittered away in such a manner. Yes, we have had many such picnics in churchyards, Edmund and I. Once, when we were out on what must have been our fifth or sixth such trip, I said to him that actually all these churches, with their exquisite medieval fittings, were ours you know, meaning Roman Catholic. My comment had been in jest but his Anglican heart had not seen the joke and he had wrestled me to the ground, sat on my stomach and held my arms down over my head hissing at me to apologize. Never at any time in my life had I felt so physically vulnerable, so I had apologized and never repeated my comment.

As we ate together I reminisced about some of the churches we had visited as I visualized his hand against the bark of the tree and the strength of his wrists as he had furiously pinioned me to the ground. What would his response be if he knew that I was poisoning him? Could he perhaps know? How had he known that yew was a poison? Why had he said that maybe he was being poisoned and then abruptly dropped the subject? Could he know? Could he? No, I thought not. He would not be sitting here beside me eating bread and cheese, responding to my memories with those of his own, surely? If he did know, would he hit me — would his right hand lift thudding against my face forcing me to lose my balance? Perhaps instead of an open hand my face would encounter a fist. If he knew of my activities I could not imagine that he would go to the police, somehow that was not his style. I had seen him angry, witnessed a cruel vengeful side to him that I found curiously surprising, strangely appealing. If he discovered that I was poisoning him he could very easily give me a thrashing and then, when I had recovered, politely resume our ritual of taking tea together on Thursday afternoons. But what if he did not want retribution, what if he looked at me in disgust and turned his back and walked away? What then? I would have to leave London. Find somewhere else to live, somewhere else to have a bookshop. But if I were successful he would never know, for he would be dead.

Penny for them, he says. I look at him, look deeply into

his eyes and I know that he does not know, and tell him that I was thinking of the different cemeteries I had been in over the years. With or without me, he asks. Both, I say. When I met you, he tells me, I thought it was weird your need to visit cemeteries, the pleasure that you gain from wandering rows of gravestones. It's morbid — even though I like to accompany you now — you do take it too far. I begin to protest but Edmund continues, talking over me. It's true, it is true. You very nearly ruined our holiday last year because you went into a state over the grave of the family killed in a car accident. Don't you remember? Yes, I remembered, I could clearly recall the grave with its circular photograph and the engraved names of father, mother, son and the same engraved date of death for all of them. They had died some way distant from where they were interred and I envisioned them setting off for — for what, for where? Had they been killed on the journey to or from? Had they died instantly or with an awareness of life ending? It seemed such a waste: two parents in their early thirties and their four-year-old son. What had been the point of their lives; so that thirty years later I could stand there and feel myself slip into a crisis about the meaningless of life? There I was: on holiday, gazing at them, a dead family. For the remainder of the visit I carried their faces with me, as Edmund and I took long walks through fields of sunflowers, past farmhouses, along the banks of looping rivers. As we drove dusty country roads I brooded over their imagined deaths, revolving scenario upon scenario in my mind, until Edmund had eventually asked in annoyance whether I wished to go home. I did not, for I felt, in fact, more at ease than I had for some time.

Edmund's voice pulls me back and I catch the end of

his sentence which he graciously repeats. He is telling me that the one thing he truly loathes about the mainland is the Catholic habit of exhibiting photographs on graves. It is, he says, not necessary. The mainland. That is my term for Europe, a term I derisively employ when talking about the island mentality of the English. If we are all Europeans, I say, with England an island, then the remainder of Europe must be the mainland, must it not? I smile at Edmund's use of my term, his adoption of my phrase as his own, and fleetingly I wonder what characteristics of his I have acquired to use as my own.

ii

In the hospital waiting room, as the smell of disinfectant singes my nostrils, I wish I had never come. I glance at Edmund cautiously. His face, pale, tense, expresses an anxiety that I reciprocate. On the return drive to London I had allowed myself to be persuaded to accompany him to his hospital appointment. He had manipulated me, played upon my relaxed mood of well-being. I was, he said, his best friend, the only person that he wanted to be with him. It was not that he actually required a companion, he went on, he could very easily get himself to and from the hospital, but he wanted someone, me, to be with him. To literally hold his hand. His doctor, bemused as to why the drugs prescribed for Edmund were ineffective, had booked him in for a gastroscopy. Which is what, I asked, surely not having something stuck up your backside? No, no, the other end, down my throat, it only takes five minutes, but he wanted my company. I didn't have to, he insisted, his face expressing neediness betrayed the casualness of his words, so I consented.

My nerves held until the moment we reached the hospital waiting room. There is something about such rooms, a combination of the smell and the strange light reflected off the faces of the doctors and nurses. Edmund sat, shuffling his legs, folding and unfolding his arms. I offered him a section of the newspaper, he declined. As I focused on the words describing the recent conviction of a woman for murder, the thought entered my mind that, with this test, the doctors might find evidence of poison in Edmund's stomach. I coughed a little, stood to say that I needed the loo. Edmund looked irritated, telling me not to be too long. In the lavatory, thick with cigarette smoke, I gazed at my face, my eyes raking my features, feeling nauseous as I breathed in the smoke. I didn't look like a murderess, did I? What then did a woman capable of killing look like? What about the girl in the paper – long blonde hair, blue eyes, pretty, long-legged, who stabbed her girlfriend not once but eighteen times. The first thrust of the knife could be explained as anger, perhaps also the second, the third, the fourth, but what of the tenth and the eleventh and so on? Could one read death in the face of a potential killer? But I was not a killer, not yet. In time. In time. Turning on the tap, I hold my hands under the cold running water, maintaining eye contact with myself in the mirror. I know that they will not find poison in Edmund's stomach, certainly no poison traceable to me. The prognosis will probably be that he has an allergy, followed by a referral to a nutritionist to monitor his diet. They will never suspect that the curly-haired, green-eyed, young woman who accompanies him is gradually poisoning him. On my return to the waiting room I take his hand which is damp and as he removes it to shed his jacket I am able to smell the pungent aroma of his armpits, secreting fear. An older woman, weeping, enters the room supported by a nurse, who informs the woman's companion that she has taken it all rather badly and that some people do, but that she will get over it after she has had a rest. Edmund watches, I watch, everyone in the waiting room watches as the distressed woman leaves, then we sit back to hide behind our newspapers and magazines.

When his name is called Edmund stands and without a look in my direction follows the nurse. He is gone for ten minutes then reappears wearing a disagreeable air, his lips pressed together are bloodless. You haven't backed out, have you, I ask. No, it's been done, I'm finished. His voice is low, slightly hoarse, can we please go home? He takes hold of my arm, lifting me from the seat and leads me out of the waiting room, away from the prodding, delving eyes of those awaiting their turn. On the short drive home he remains hunched in the corner of his seat, face turned away looking out of the window. I ask none of the questions that clog my throat desperate for air. At his flat he pulls an armchair over near the windows through which a fragile sunlight trickles and there he sits, eyes closed, absorbing the sun, perched like an old man upon a park bench.

I have no idea what to do with myself. He does not wish me to leave, nor does he wish for tea or food. He requires nothing but my silent presence. I retreat to the sofa, curling up in a corner, legs folded beneath me, making a pretence of reading the stack of magazines that have accumulated on a side table, flicking through them, unable to focus, but it gives my hands a sense of something to do, and I know that the rustle of the turning page is penetrating his ear, reassuring him of my presence. Finally it is I who succumbs to the need for a cup of tea and I place Edmund's precariously on the side of his chair and retreat once more to the sofa balancing my cup on my knees. He picks up his cup coming to sit beside me then stares into the depths of his elderflower tea — *sans* poison — and I wonder what it is that he sees as the steam swirls upwards dampening his face. Whatever it is does not please him for suddenly he lifts his face and the cup, flinging it towards the wall: it misses, but bounces against the rug, tea darkening its vibrant red.

I sit quietly beside him. Not a movement, absolute stillness. Only when he leans his head into his hands and begins to weep, his fingertips savagely pressing his eyeballs backwards into his skull, do I move, setting my teacup down on the floor before turning to pull his unresisting head down into my lap. As he continues to weep I lay my hand on his head, my fingers sifting his hair. In the years that I have known Edmund I have never seen him cry, I have witnessed all manner of his moods — including the throwing of teacups — but never tears. When more calm he tells me of his trauma at the hospital. The cold anaesthetic spray on his throat, the tiny camera on the end of rubber tubing sliding down his throat; the dry retching that had started immediately as his gullet had desperately tried to rid itself of this foreign object; the sound of the doctor's voice pleasantly chatting about Edmund's grandmother, Hermione, and how he loved her books; the three biting pains as parts of his stomach lining was pecked away, as if by a trapped bird, to be taken for analysis; then as the tubing was removed and he had sat up the doctor had handed him a copy of his own book on Hermione and asked him to sign it, which he had done. It was over, finished. He was expected to get down off the table and expected to go back out into the world as if his innards had not just been vandalized.

He sat up now, swollen-eyed, snuffling. Somehow I expected him to be embarrassed by his tears, instead he seemed refreshed as he blew his nose. Following his outbursts in the past he had always been mortified, apologetic, but not now. He looked at me and slipping an arm around my shoulder said that he needed some affection, so I shifted my position to put my arms around him and we held each other for some time. I allowed him to play with my neck, his fingers kneading the skin, sliding up into my curls to rub my skull bones. I tolerated his hand stroking the skin at the back of my knee but as his hand slid up my thigh I placed my hand on his, and pulled back to stare at him as I said no. Please, he said. No. Please. No. Yes. No.

Not after all these years, Edmund, it would be ridiculous. He moved his hands to hold my face, thumbs stroking, pressing into my cheekbones, his head moving towards mine to catch my lip with his teeth and bite, a sharp nip. Please, I want to. But I don't want to, I am thinking as he continues to hold my face, fingertips brushing my jawline. This is madness, I think as I watch him reach down and undo my shoe laces and slide my feet free. This should not happen, this must not happen, I say as his hand slides under my skirt, fingers moving inside the waistband of my leggings to take them down, pulling so that my legs are suddenly bare and the cool air hitting them gives me goosebumps. I can't do this, I am about to say as his fingers find the crotch of my knickers pressing, playing through the cotton. I was poisoning the man, I couldn't fuck him as well, could I? It seemed, though, that I was, for I unbuttoned his trousers and opened his shorts to get his penis out, swallowing a nervous urge to giggle. To hide my smirk I stood over him to remove my knickers and having done so, as I began to lower myself, he stopped me, lifting my skirt to rub his face against my pubic hair. His lips moved along the top of my thighs as his hands spread my legs further allowing his tongue to probe my vagina, parting and delving. I felt myself moistening and tilted my hips to give him better access, giving into the pleasure, curling my toes into the soft fabric of the sofa, wondering who it is that has taken Edmund in hand in recent years and given him lessons in oral sex. Briefly, I become aware that I might actually enjoy this as I feel the tension congealing around my hips and groin to join with the ache stretching from pubic bone to sphincter muscles, then Edmund's face reappears and holding my hips he guides me downwards. I open myself with my fingers so that he can enter me, then, all my desire vanished, I sit astride him, enclosing him, moving slightly. By closing my eyes I avoid his gaze but move my face closer to his inhaling deeply through my nostrils to enjoy the smell of myself on his face. This smell becomes my focus as does the roughness of his trousers abrasive against the skin of my legs and buttocks, while his stammered breath hits my ear. Mechanically I move along that length of flesh, again and again, relentlessly up then down. Will he never come? My thighs begin to ache with the strain and just as it is on the tip of my tongue to say get on with it, he does so. Through my eyelashes I watch the contortions of his face with a benign curiosity as I feel him stiffen inside me and strain and finally come. His grip immobilizes me as he murmurs thank you into my ear, my neck, against my mouth, while his semen trickles out of me and down my thigh where it quickly dries.

Every word I read pressed into my brain as if upon a bruise, and although filled with foreboding at the response that I will trigger in myself, I read on, feeling the ice-cold water of apprehension and alarm drip into my bowels and finally overflow. I read how Sarah Metyard and her daughter, also called Sarah, were tried in 1762 and found guilty of the murder of one of their thirteen-year-old apprentices, Ann Naylor. While the Metyard women ran their haberdashery business, Ann and other girls were employed to take care of the household chores. Ann's completion of the tasks assigned to her did not please the Metyard women and their initial punishments were to beat her and deprive her of food. When her response had been to run away she was found and forcibly returned to the household where the violence accelerated.

On her return the Metyard women took Ann to a bedroom where they battered her with a broomstick; following this they tied her to a door with her hands fastened behind her so that she could neither sit nor lie down and they kept her in this position of forced standing for three days. During this period the other female apprentices would take their work so as to be beside Ann and, as they later testified in court, by the third day she was dead. When the Metyard women were informed of this, the younger Sarah attempted to pound some life back into Ann by using her shoe. But when this proved fruitless, Ann was untied and carried to a garret bedroom. Two days later the women concocted the story that Ann had recovered from her injuries to run away. The details of Ann's disappearance came out, however, when Sarah Metyard the younger divulged the true sequence of events to her lover.

As the other apprentices had correctly guessed, Ann Naylor had indeed been dead after being tied to the door for three days. Sarah the elder had refused to give the girl a burial because it was obvious that she had been treated brutally and starved. Moving Ann's body to another garret room the Metyard mother and daughter stuffed her remains into a box, where they were kept for two months until eventually the stench became unbearable. Sarah the elder then took Ann's decomposing body from the box and, despite the maggots feeding upon the flesh, proceeded to cut it to pieces; removing the arms, the legs from the knee down, the hands, and the head. Her first thought was to burn the pieces in the fireplace but sickened at the smell of burning flesh which permeated the room she wrapped the remainder of the body parts in bedclothes which she then disposed of in a local ditch.

Informed of this, young Sarah's lover was horrified and proceeded to notify the local constabulary. By lamplight they collected the scattered body parts of Ann Naylor which, despite the winter cold, had become rankly putrescent. The pieces were taken to the workhouse where the coroner unwrapped them, washed them in a tub of water to rid them of dirt and maggots, then laid them out on a board where, in the best manner possible, they were assembled to form a young girl's body. At this point I felt the contents of my gut lift and hesitantly flop back into place. In my mind is the image of a photograph that I had seen in a book, of an armless and legless torso laid out on an autopsy table. A grainy black–and–white image taken in the early 1930s, poorly reproduced. I had stood in some bookshop staring first at the torso, then to the left at the accompanying photograph of the smiling woman whose body it was, whose body it had once been, that now lay on cold steel. Then my eyes had shifted to the right to the photograph of a different woman, she who had dismembered the body of her friend, before stuffing it into a travelling trunk. I had examined her face at length before my fingers hurriedly flicked the pages to cover the torso's nakedness and I moved away to run my eyes over other books. Despite my distaste for that image I was drawn back to the book again and again, impelled to lift it and open it at the page where the body was displayed. That was what I visualized: that woman's body, hacked to pieces by Winnie Ruth Judd in 1931. One woman disposing of another, just as Sarah Metyard had disposed of Ann Naylor. The Metyard women had been hanged but Winnie Ruth had been sent to a mental institution from which she had been released, fit and well, to live within the community, in 1971.

I resurface from that mental image to find myself staring at the computer screen, seeing neither the screen nor the words upon it. I blink to refocus on the objects scattered over my desk, imprinting their tangibility upon my retina to block the visual echo within my mind's eye. As my customers approach to ask me questions, questions which I normally find tiresome, instead of my normal obstructive manner I am more than usually helpful, eager to engage in conversation.

I avoid the box of books which remains to be catalogued, glancing into its depth periodically as I pass to see whether the contents have somehow diminished without my assistance. I tidy the bookshelves, realign spines which do not require my touch, arms folded I stand in the doorway watching the world pass by.

Ultimately, with resignation, I resume my position at my desk, unable to think of another way to assuage the apprehension that has arisen in me.

My hand reaches into the box and lifts out three books, stamped in gold on their green spine with the date 1767. All concern the trial of Elizabeth Brownrigg for the murder of her apprentice Mary Clifford. Brownrigg was a highly esteemed midwife, so respected for her skills that the London parish of St Dunstan's-in-the-West had appointed her the official midwife to look after destitute women in labour. Elizabeth herself had given birth to fifteen children, of whom only three survived, and was said to be the epitome of kindness and understanding in her midwifery practice. So large had her practice grown that she required the assistance of apprentices, provided in the shape of poor young girls from the workhouse. At first she treated her apprentices with a similar kindness to that with which she tended her pregnant charges, but almost overnight this changed, with no apparent reason for the reversal of her temperament and decline into sadism.

Elizabeth had obtained her first apprentice in May 1765 and a month later her cruelties begin. Eight weeks later the girl escapes and makes an official complaint to the authorities saying she had been whipped while naked and that on other occasions, when fault was found with her work, Elizabeth had dunked her head in a pail of dirty water and threatened to drown her. Despite this complaint, Elizabeth has no difficulty in acquiring the services of a further two apprentices, Mary Mitchell in December 1765 and Mary Clifford in February 1766.

Some months pass before Mary Clifford's condition is discovered by her mother who is accompanied by the local authorities. Her condition shocks the assembled group: her back and shoulders are cut, her head wounded with many bloody gashes, as are her hips, legs and thighs. Her face and throat are bruised and swollen, and her mouth distended to such a degree that she cannot close her lips. When she attempts to speak she can only make inarticulate noises in her throat. She and Mary Mitchell, whose condition is only slightly less terrible, are removed from the Brownrigg residence and placed in hospital.

Elizabeth's husband, James Brownrigg, is arrested and taken before a magistrate, but Elizabeth herself has fled in the company of her eldest son. An advertisement is placed in the newspapers offering a reward for their capture, a reward which will double the following day when Mary Clifford dies. Within days Elizabeth and her son have been arrested, after a sharp-eyed landlord saw through the disguises of his two most recent lodgers. At the trial Mary Mitchell, still recovering from her own wounds, is the chief witness both to her own treatment and to that which had killed Mary Clifford.

She informs the court how Elizabeth had beaten them both with the stump of a riding whip and on many occasions when their wounds had only just begun to heal and scab over she would beat them again so that their wounds would reopen to bleed afresh. In conclusion she told how a hook had been tied to a beam in the kitchen to which Elizabeth had tied them in turn, after forcing them to remove their clothes, then thrashed them till they bled. The final beating had occurred on the day prior to the arrival of the authorities when Mary Clifford had been tied naked to the hook and beaten five times within the one day. When she had cried out in pain Elizabeth had cut her tongue and mouth with a pair of scissors.

Throughout her trial Elizabeth agreed only in part to the charge against her, in that while she did not deny having beaten both girls, her intent had not been, at any time, to kill Mary Clifford. In the process she acquitted her husband and son of any involvement, and thus while she was found guilty and sentenced to hang, they were merely fined and given brief prison sentences.

My brow is locked into a frown as I look at the pile of books on the Elizabeth Brownrigg trial. The question of why she behaved as she did will never be answered, can only remain suspended in time. Was it merely about power? Had Elizabeth Brownrigg and the Sarahs Metyard behaved with such cruelty only because it was possible for them to do so? Was it purely callousness? Indifference?

Yet again I am reminded of a photograph, one that I had seen in a newspaper, in an article narrating one of the interminable African civil wars, of a body lying beside a half-dried-up pond of water, a naked body, a dead body. A body that had been skinned as the final indignity to be heaped upon whatever brutality had caused its death. I had looked and felt the palms of my hands begin to sweat and my knees weaken, although I had been seated, and blinked at the body that had been so carefully stripped of its skin that what remained somehow resembled a peeled gooseberry with the delicate veins apparent in the flesh of the fruit. Only in this case the flesh was red and the veins threading the flesh had once moved blood from limb to limb.

Now years after seeing that photograph I sit and try to imagine the physical act of skinning a body alive, or beating someone so that their scabs are ripped open and begin to bleed, or forcing open someone's mouth to cut their tongue with scissors, but I am unable to maintain indifference and feel my heart constrict and cold sweat spread along the crease of my buttocks. What separates me from those atrocities? I am poisoning Edmund, am I not? Poisoning him with deliberate cruelty, watching him suffer, taking pleasure from his pain. My inhumanity is equal to theirs. I feel the moisture intensify and the dampness spread so that I am sure that as I stand my trousers will reveal a wet patch. I avoid looking at my two customers who are ignorant of the trembling in my limbs. What am I going to do? My breath is becoming more laboured, my pulse is beginning to race. Any moment now I know that I am going to crumple in a moaning heap, or start screaming, or begin to bang my head against the wall, anything to allay the tremendous pressure growing in my chest, anything to still the wind whining through the cavities of my skull. My hands shake as they grip the desk and on their backs I can see every hair, each fine line, each pore of my skin as if it were enlarged under a magnifying glass. I look at my fingers and see them peeled of a layer of flesh revealing their insides.

I must get out of the bookshop before I go mad. In the past I have always managed to stay in control no matter how panic-stricken I have become, but there is always a first time for hysterics. I listen to my voice politely saying that I am closing for lunch and am aware of two pairs of eyes turning my way. They both leave with ill grace, nothing is more hostile than an interrupted book browser, and I follow them through the door remembering to turn the closed sign. Briskly I stride down the street somehow managing to hold myself back from running, I must not run for that would only exacerbate the racing of my heart.

On the corner of Marylebone Road I stop, digging my

heels into the footpath, willing myself to remain stationary as I calculate how easy it would be to slip under the spinning wheels of an oncoming car, to be crushed, to hear one's own bones crack. But I do not wish to die. Oblivion and nothingness, yes; death, no. Yet there is a part of me that is drawn to those wheels, that can feel myself sliding beneath them. I try to calm myself, breathing in deeply through my nostrils and slowly exhaling, aware that people are watching me out of the corner of their eyes. I sense their wariness, I can see how I must appear to them in my mind's eye: skin tightly accentuating the contours of my facial bones, waxen with a slight sheen. For although I am cold, am shivering, I am also sweating, dread oozing from my pores.

I stand on the corner of Marylebone Road reeking of fear. Unable to trust myself not to plunge into the oncoming traffic I suddenly veer to the left, avoiding the eyes that glance at me curiously then slide away disinclined to meet my manic gaze. My walking run quickly gets me to the park, where in the rose garden I clamber through some shrubs to sit underneath a tree, my back against the trunk. I am hidden here, totally secreted away. I could die and no one would find me. Yet I cannot relax, cannot ease the tightness in my chest, nor the shaking of my limbs. As the bile rises in my throat to fill my mouth, I choke a little as I heave and spit, its rancidness burning the back of my throat and up my nasal passage, bringing weak tears to my eyes. I curl up on my side, tightly into a ball, ignoring the damp of the grass and the earth seeping through my clothes and into my bones. I rock myself from side to side and slowly the motion of my body soothes my mind.

Walking slowly I approach the shop, every tiny noise jarring the interior of my head. So absorbed am I in placing one foot in front of the other that I am unprepared for the sight of Edmund sitting on the doorstep reading, awaiting me. Please God, why now? He looks up from his book and, noticing my approach, stands to meet me.

Where on earth have you been? I've been so worried. It's not like you to go off and leave the shop. Is everything all right? And so on and so forth. Clenching my jaw I wish he would bugger off and leave me alone, and in the silence that ensues I realize that I've spoken aloud, and he is standing there clutching his book to his chest and presenting his hurt face. Fuck him, I think. I won't, will not, apologize. What is it, he asks. I felt ill, I went out. For two hours? Please go, I plead in my head, but he does not read my mind. Edmund, what do you want? His eyes narrow slightly as if he is not sure how to respond. We always see each other on Thursday, he tells me. It isn't Thursday, is it? Edmund watches me. What expressions can he see flitting across my face? Resignedly, I apologize for my forgetfulness and invite him in for tea.

Upstairs neither of us mentions the visit to the hospital nor our encounter afterwards. In the kitchen I prepare the tea as Edmund settles himself in an armchair where he can partially view my movements. I am deliberately casual in every gesture I make. Opening the refrigerator I remove the foil-wrapped rhododendron, masking the action with my body. I hear him shift, and turn to look over my shoulder to check that he has not decided to join me in the kitchen; then I carefully unwrap the rhododendron bells and place them in a small amount of water in a saucepan and bring them to the boil then turn them down to simmer, watching the twelve bell-shaped flowers slowly lose their shape to form a soggy mass in the bottom of the pan. Making the appropriate noises in response to Edmund's conversation, I take the eyedropper and fill it with the liquid from the pan, although I only intend to use two drops. The remnants I tip down the sink, running the tap at full force to wash away the evidence.

What are you doing in there, he calls. I turn and smile and say that the tea is coming. Despite my earlier panic I am continuing with my plan. I turn back to the cups and pressing the rubber end of the dropper between my fingertips I squirt two droplets of odourless liquid into the bottom of Edmund's cup, then carrying the tray through to where he sits, I fill his cup with lemon verbena tea and hand it to him. I make a pretence of sipping mine and watch until he finishes his cup, then I yawn loudly, without covering my mouth. My panic attack has left me depleted, requiring sleep. I tell Edmund that I need to rest and ask him to let himself out when he has finished. Exhausted I get to the top of the stairs and lie on my bed fully clothed.

Downstairs, through my drowsiness, I hear Edmund rinsing the cups and his murmured dialogue with the cats, followed by the clatter of tins as he feeds them, his approaching footsteps on the spiral staircase, then the click of the bedroom light as he walks over to me. Bending down he unlaces my shoes, removes my socks, then undoes the belt of my trousers and pulls them off. Knickers off, cardigan off, shirt, bra, all off. I keep my head turned, hidden in the crook of my arm, away from the light which is too sharp for my eyes. I wait, listening for the sound of Edmund removing his clothes, and I wait. I peep from under my arm at him as he stands over me, studying my naked body. Still I wait. Then he takes my pyjamas and clothes me in them, sliding on the pyjama pants, doing up the buttons of the shirt. And then I am crawling along the bed and sliding between the sheets and Edmund is pulling the covers up to my chin. As he bends towards me his lips brush mine and he straightens and walks away, switching off the light. I listen as he makes his way down the spiral staircase, listen to his farewells to the cats, listen to his footsteps down yet another flight of stairs, then the bang of the bookshop door as he closes it behind him. I listen to his footsteps fade as he walks away up the road. For some hours I lie awake, listening.

Of that first year after Mary's death I remember little. I seemed to spend entire days lying on my bed, gazing out of the window and listening: to the rain on the roof, the wind in the trees, Lucille and Ella's movements from room to room. Listening for Mary. I lay and watched the seasons pass by and for the first time in my life, the only time in my life, I did not read, was unable to read. I would open a book and read the first word, the first paragraph, the first page, but unable to maintain the momentum I would lay the book aside and return to gazing out of the window. The books that I had desperately coveted, and been able to purchase with the money I had inherited from Mary's life insurance and accidental death policies, lay unread. I thought about Mary anticipating with such clarity her own death that she had insured her life not once but twice, in order to provide for me. Lucille was to get the house and land, while I received enough money to ensure that I did not need to do anything, but lie on my bed and read, for many years to come. I was in shock. What did one spend money on apart from books? Books that were now incapable of holding my attention.

Then one afternoon, my thoughts ranged as far as England, mentally exploring the country of Mary's childhood, the place she had lived for the first nineteen years of her life, and although I could not visualize myself there I knew that I would go to England, that over the past year all my listening and dream-like gazing had been a slow approach towards an image that hovered on the periphery of my vision, that had made itself known only when I was ready to see it. My decision made I left three weeks later, taking the train to Sydney, then flying on to London, using the money that I had been left by Mary. In retrospect what an audacious act it seems, I who had never travelled anywhere on my own, nor been abroad, nor on an aeroplane. Did I calm my nerves with the thought that it was only to be a visit, a summer at the most? To be truthful I don't remember, so many summers on.

I travelled at night, I have always preferred to, even as a child with Mackie and Mary, I preferred to leave and arrive at my destination while it was enwrapped in darkness. To sleep with unknown sounds and smells permeating my consciousness, awakening to a new place as if newly born.

On my first April morning in London it rained, a sleety, ice-filled rain, everything glistened, electric lights bouncing off wet surfaces to dispel the gloom. I walked in Hyde Park on that first day, huddled in layer upon layer of clothing, ill equipped for the bitter dampness. I watched in amusement that bordered on amazement as a scattering of men and women jogged around the duck pond baring unshivering arms and legs to the cold. I found a room in which to live, a box-shaped room containing a bed, a sink, a kettle, a hot plate to cook upon, and a table for the secondhand manual typewriter which I was to purchase. In those early spring days my room was cold and damp and as the weather slowly warmed, the room grew stuffy and retained the heat. Days evolved into weeks where I did little more than read, sit at the typewriter attempting to write my novel, and explore the many bookshops that beckoned from every other street. As the weather began to improve I took a notebook to the park and found the most sheltered place possible to curl up in the full beam of the sun's rays, soaking up their warmth like an old cat. Just as I was growing accustomed to their comfort and began to think that I might, after all, remove my cardigan, the sun disappeared and the world was cold once more.

During the cold months I remained in my room, writing in bed, virtually smothered by layers of clothes and blankets, hemmed in by hot water bottles in a futile attempt to retain my body warmth. I developed a chest infection and unable to rise from my bed would lean over the side to cough up tablespoonfuls of phlegm into a soup bowl. A small saucepan sat beneath the bed for when I needed to pee, unable, as I was, to make the trek down the dark hall to the lavatory that I shared with three other people. Many days passed before I realized that I required a doctor. Awkwardly I removed myself from bed to call for a taxi to take me to the hospital. There I waited for three hours, coughing my phlegm into the paper bowl provided for me, before a doctor tapped me on the chest, took my pulse and temperature, and then wrote out a slip of paper for antibiotics. He had hardly said a word beyond the questions to confirm the details on the form that I had given the nurse. The cold detachment of the English, of which I had heard, was not exaggerated. After filling my prescription I returned to my room and wept. I wanted Mary, even Lucille would do. By the third day I felt ready to rise and heat a tin of soup which I devoured with slightly mould-speckled bread. Within an hour I had vomited, but I was on my way to recovery.

The warm weeks of summer seemed to have hardly begun before once again they had finished. Feeling cheated as the evenings began to draw in earlier and earlier, I came to fear the gradual lessening of light and would try to be ensconced in my room before dark, nervous of entering an eclipsed room, which daily grew more frigid. That I left the curtains open, allowing the cold to seep through the panes of glass, only exacerbated the lack of warmth, but occupying a lightless room depressed me and I relied upon the street to irradiate the room as I slept. I exhausted my days in the warmth of the library, in trepidation watching the clock for when I would have to return to my dreaded room. As winter deepened the light lessened until it seemed as if the world existed solely in a smothered halflight, sky merging with city. I contemplated returning to Webster Creek but although enticed by the prospect of sun, the thought of losing the plethora of bookshops I had discovered, of never again meandering the length of Charing Cross Road, was beyond imagining.

Armoured in a long coat, boots, scarf, hat and gloves, I set off in search of a new room, a warm room, in which to live. My explorations took me to the boundaries of the city, into the suburbs, but the cramped rows of terraced houses induced in me a sense of claustrophobia, so endlessly did they stretch, streets without end.

It was on returning from one of these forays that I stumbled upon St Marylebone Row, having taken the wrong exit from the train station. There I stood, on a day so grey and damp that I could almost see the moisture in the air, feeling the corners of my mouth tugged upward in pleasure as I took in the bookshops lining first one side of the street then the other. It was, it remains so today, one of those eccentric

London streets that is tucked away behind others, hidden, practically forgotten, unmarked on the map. As the air reddened my nose I surmised that I would require at least a day to explore this haven, time that this day no longer contained. Now, I was cold and damp and required a whisky with green ginger wine to fortify me for my roomward trek.

I walked into an empty pub and tucked myself in a corner, sipping my drink and reading my book, the heat of the whisky bathing the rawness of my chest, dulling my cough. Slowly the pub filled and trapped in my corner I surreptitiously eavesdropped on the conversations taking place around my head. Quickly I deciphered that the gathered individuals were the booksellers from St Marylebone Row and I avidly listened to their discussions of books and each other. They were drily witty, bitingly sarcastic, their words like scalpels cutting through each other and the world at large. Anyone who dared not to agree with a proferred opinion was deemed a fool, anyone who was not a bookseller was automatically thought to be a fool. I hid my reactions to their comments behind my book which I held up before my face as if I were reading. I strained my hearing further when I heard a voice say that it had still not had an offer on the bookshop he wished to sell. I peeped over the edge of my book, looking for the person to accompany the cut-glass accent, a voice that seemed estranged from its owner when I realized it belonged to the body of an ageing hippy who appeared to be near the end of his trail, greasy hair curled down his back and the spectacles that repeatedly slid down his oily nose were pushed back into place by black-encrusted fingernails. This was a bookseller? Those hands handled books? I glanced at the others, a cross section of inhumanity: young and old, men and women, but all predominantly plain. Contemplating them I felt attractive, felt that maybe amongst this assemblage of ordinaries I might possibly find a place. For they all wore the slightly retarded, inward look with which I associated the bookish.

The following day I returned to St Marylebone Row accompanied by my first hangover, for I had sat in the pub sipping whiskies with green ginger until closing. I arrived with an incipient nausea swimming in my stomach and dodgy bowels, not to speak of a headache that prodded my brain with massive thumbs. The taste of whisky clung to my tongue and the fumes still burned my nostrils.

I wandered in and out of bookshops feeling desperately ill, convinced that at any moment I was going to die, or at least pass out, unable to appreciate the diversity of books desperate to fall from the shelves into my waiting hands. In the middle, opposite me, was 'R. Hare' with a For Sale sign propped up in the window. I crossed to peer over railings to the basement entrance that was lined with plastic rubbish bins all missing their lids. The shop looked closed, there was no sign on the door specifying one way or the other, and a blind had been pulled down to cover the glass. Taking hold of the handle I pushed, expecting to meet resistance, and virtually fell through the door, to be thumped in the face by a cloud of cigarette smoke. I felt the water rush into my mouth and swallowed hard repeatedly although my stomach contained nothing to regurgitate, having rid itself of its contents earlier in the morning. Are you open I asked, focusing on the figure just decipherable in the haze of smoke. It would appear so, he said. I scrutinized the room, eyes moving over bookshelves on the point of collapse, so crowded were they. Books in teetering stacks obscuring lower shelves, books jumbled in boxes one on top of the other. It was excruciating, unbearable. The room had no natural light, bookcases obscured the front and rear windows with a single naked bulb inadequately lighting the room. I couldn't bring myself to touch a single book, I wished I had never entered this depressing place.

As I turned to leave, my coat caught the edge of a pile of books, which tumbled to the floor. Without even looking in my direction he snidely intoned, if you can't handle the books properly fucking well leave. How dare you speak to me that way, I said. We both appeared taken aback that I had responded. I coughed, every hack sawing through my temples. Look at the state this bookshop is in, look at the books, are you surprised no one will buy it from you? He regarded me carefully through the cigarette smoke. You buy it then, he sneered. How much, I asked. He named his price, I told him not to be ridiculous, and offered him somewhat less. He took a long puff of his cigarette before he agreed. We stared at each other, neither knowing the next move to make. He broke the silence by saying that if I still wished to purchase the bookshop I should return in one week and then we would talk business.

When I returned a week later the For Sale sign was still in place. I carried with me a long list of questions that the bank required answers to before they would give me a mortgage. The bank manager had been suspicous; why did Mr Hare wish to sell the business for so little, something must be terribly, terribly wrong. Over a pub lunch Mr Hare, whose name was actually Marcus Emmeline, told me why he wished to sell at such a knock-down price. He was bored, he said. If he had sold one book he had sold them all. He wanted to go to Morocco and laze in the sun smoking hashish, sleeping with whatever boy took his fancy. He had been a diplomatic brat, sent back to boarding school in England while his parents moved every two years; following school he had declined university, travelling instead, getting himself into all manner of scrapes which his father's connections solved. In despair his parents had bought R. Hare for him in the hope that he would settle and for seven years he had, but enough was enough. When I told him that he was not as old as I had thought, he had responded that his face expressed the many pleasures that he had packed into his few years.

The following week I returned again. A surveyor, whose services I had located in the telephone book, accompanied me at the request of the bank. If the building was in sound condition they had agreed to provide me with half the required sum, the other half I would obtain from Mary's money. Two weeks later I returned with a solicitor who had drawn up the transfer of freehold papers. One month later R. Hare was officially mine; I had a home as well as a shop full of books. I was a bookseller. It was all so ludicrously easy.

During the month that I waited to take up residence I haunted other bookshops absorbing details and features that I would notate and grandiosely expand on paper in preparation for the opening of R. Hare. I memorized the mannerisms and gestures of the booksellers, practising facial postures in front of the mirror. I longed to talk to Mary to be reassured that in buying R. Hare I had done the correct thing, instead I telephoned Lucille and her non-committal support allowed that if it didn't work I could always sell up and come home. At her utterance of the word home, I knew that Webster Creek was no longer home, I had no home, R. Hare was all that I had, so that on the day I was due to arrive to collect the keys I was there early. As I pushed open the door I was swamped with such a deep sense of *déjà vu* that I stumbled as I moved forwards breathing in cigarette smoke. In one hand Marcus held a battered suitcase, in the other he proffered a key-ring from which dangled three keys for the front door, all the other keys for the building were in their appropriate locks. I took the keys in my hand, their metallic coldness seeping into my palm, up my arm, past my elbow to my shoulder and making the skin of my neck tingle. With a nod he was gone, stepping past me out of the door to which I had moved in order to watch him disappear around the corner.

I never saw him again, never spoke with him, will probably never know what became of him. Seven years after buying R. Hare he left, without a last word to the other booksellers he had known over the years. Occasionally there are sightings of him, reports of his death, but who knows, I'm sure if we actually saw him in the street we would not even recognize him, not because he has changed but because our visual memories of him have grown so distorted.

After he had disappeared from view I closed the door and picked my way through piles of books to tiptoe up the spiral staircase and stand in my sitting room, weaving past boxes of books to open the windows, and up the next set of stairs to do the same. I had already given notice to quit my bedsit and needed to return only to put my few belongings into a taxi for the move to be complete. In the following days I engaged in imaginary conversations with Mary as to what tasks I must do to organize my household, but I avoided touching the boxes of books which required sorting. I put the task off and off and off, going on shopping expeditions to furnish my rooms above the shop, while the bookshop itself remained closed and airless. I bought a car, ostensibly to be able to rid myself of the boxes of books which I considered unsellable. Instead as the days grew longer and warmer I took myself off into the countryside and would return with my own boxes of books with which I planned to fill the shelves of R. Hare when I had cleared the space. This went on and on, the summer passing in a splendid haze of countryside and book buying, the only dark spot in each day being the few minutes it took me to traverse the shop on my way out and upon my return. I developed a habit of visiting village churches, I liked to wander in graveyards looking for the surname Miss. As I meandered I raked my memory for details of Mary's life, but the harder I searched, prodding distant conversations for hints and clues to where exactly she was from, the less I could actually remember her ever saying about herself. I knew of course that I could go to the Public Record Office and look out the details of her birth, or telephone Lucille and ask her to find Mary's birth certificate, but I didn't want to. I wanted to stumble upon a headstone, in a quiet country churchyard complete with ancient yew, that is engraved with my Christian name, the surname of my mother, my grandparents. Never yet have I found it. I mulled over the possibility that Mary's parents might still be alive and began to vet old faces that I encountered, searching for vague resemblances, finding none. It is possible of course that I have seen them, an old man, an old woman, and not recognized them at all.

Then one night I had a dream, or early one morning I should say. I dreamt that I was in a place where Mary was which seemed far away, but wherever I was, I was sad and mourning, even though Mary was there. My sense of loss was not for a person or for people but for books and streets and rain, and for all the walks in the rain through the streets to a bookshop, where a fire burned, that I had taken. Upon awakening I found the street glistening, shining from the rain that drifted silkily, softly down upon it. I dressed and made myself a pot of tea and took it downstairs to the bookshop and began the task that I had delayed for so many months. I removed the books and dismantled the shelves that blocked the rear window, which I then cleaned; the following day I did the front, so that by the third day at least I had natural light and was able to begin slowly sorting through the stacked piles and boxes of books. To me there seemed to be little of value, but I was very aware that what I thought rubbish might be another reader's treasure. As I sorted I set aside the trivia that I found marking pages, old bookmarks, postcards, stamps, pressed flowers, bus tickets, tickets from concerts and plays, the occasional photograph. I kept them to frame. The books that I did not want I tried to give to charity shops but not even they wanted them and I was forced to take them to the municipal dump and pay to leave them to be destroyed. I refilled the shop with the books that I had purchased, arranging and rearranging until they rested in an appropriate place.

On the morning of my opening I stood in R. Hare, arms nervously hugging my waist. What if no one came through the door? But the weather was on my side, it rained, a fine non-stop drizzle, that forced people in to shelter, to scan my shelves. The other booksellers on St Marylebone Row came to shake my hand and wish me good luck, nodding in approval at the transformation I had wrought. Casually they evaluated my stock and my prices, as well, of course, as myself.

My open Australian manner took them off guard; it is a characteristic I have lost over the years, along with my accent, I am now as secretive, as cold, as fraudulent in my friendliness as any Englishman or woman, having mastered the ability to sound sincere while practising the art of being obstructive. I was naïve on that first day and for many days that followed, marking the spot for all the knives that were sharpened to be plunged into my back the minute that it was turned. But as I turned the closed sign at the end of the first day I stood in the darkness to watch the reflection of my gas fire flickering in my bookshop window, and if not exactly content nor was I discontent.

In the fourteenth week of my bookselling career I sat with a letter from Ella, which I read in a fragmentary fashion between tending to my customers and answering their every question, for I had not yet developed the knack of the polite brush-off. I read of her decision to join the church, snickering at the thought of cosmetically enhanced Ella in a habit and a veil but my smile turned rictus the further I read, for she was asking if she could visit me following a pilgrimage to Lisieux. With dread I acquiesced, but in the end she didn't come. Postcards informed me that she had decided to extend her European tour to encompass the pilgrimage route through France to Santiago de Compostela and then move on to Rome. Before she left Rome I attempted to telephone her only to be told that there was no nun named Ella resident in the convent. Yet my message had got through, for within half an hour Ella had returned my call, politely reminding me that she was now Sister Martin. When I had responded that I continued to think of her as Ella she told me that when she had taken the veil she felt that Ella had been laid to rest and that Sister Martin had been born in her place, and that it was solely as Sister Martin that she saw herself.

Periodically she comes to visit, arriving with no warning, staying for an afternoon on her way to some pilgrimage site or another, and as the years have passed I too have come to think of her as Sister Martin, for Ella she is not. And I recall how desperately as a child I had wanted Ella to disappear, and now she has.

I remember one sunny Saturday afternoon how, while browsing at the newsagent's, I had been attracted by the lurid words on the cover of a True Crime magazine and picking it up had flicked through it nonchalantly. For some obscure reason I had been too embarrassed to appear engrossed, but with the new issue the following month, I bought a copy, replete with stories of bodies and body parts strewn in bizarre and not-so-bizarre places. I hid it to read in secret at my leisure. Month after month my secret pile of True Crime magazines grew, and I became convinced that the entire world consisted of those who murdered and those who were murdered; those who did it, and those who had it done to them, and I took to examining faces, trying to divide those I encountered into the two groups.

Then one day I read an article concerning a girl who had disappeared. Such a story was not an unusual feature of each issue, only this time my eye had been captured by her photograph, that of a pretty blonde child who so resembled Ella, that I compared her face against a photograph of Ella that I had pilfered from Lucille's photo album. As I read the story of this girl who had disappeared never to be seen again the thought formed in my mind that Ella had that look. The look of the missing, the disappeared, the murdered. I knew that if I wished hard enough, prayed hard enough, it might also happen to her, that one day she would be there, and then not. And it happened. Not in the way that I thought it would, but Ella no longer exists.

SIX

I approach the bed in slow motion, wading through space, through time, my footfalls keeping pace with the blood pulse in my head. I approach the bed on which Edmund lies naked, arms by his side, hands turned upwards, fingers folded inwards seeking tender palms. I approach the bed on which Edmund lies awaiting my approach. I stand over him, who lies there, and despite his unclothedness, the bareness of his skin to the air and to my gaze, my eyes remain fixed on his face. His already slender face which has become even more so in the recent weeks. Skin tightening to enhance brow bone and cheekbones, flesh recessing into eye sockets, eyeballs bulbous. Edmund's face. My eyes linger, straining for the slightest movement, a quivering eyelash, the flare of a nostril on inhalation then exhalation of breath. Without thought my hand lifts to touch his cheek, fingers trembling against skin. But as my hand falls away to rest at my side I see the imprint of my fingers survive on his cheek as if I had struck him a blow. It is my eyelids and lashes that quiver as my eyes remain fixed on this mark, watching it grow harsher, darker, suffusing with blood, wine red, turning plum and darkening further to black. A purplescent black that strains and pushes against the skin of his cheek until it begins to seep delicately through the pores of his skin. I watch, not as it should, the blood running down the side of Edmund's cheek towards the hairline to be absorbed onto the pillow upon which his head is laid, but as the blood trickles inwards to encounter the line of his nose, running along and then upwards to engulf his eye socket before cascading over the bridge of his nose to inundate the other socket. At that moment I become aware that he is watching me, that his eyelids have opened and his brown eyes are looking directly into mine. As his eyelids lower, lashes spiky wet with blood, I awaken, wrenched into an upright position.

Beside me Edmund turns, placing the flat of his hand on the base of my spine, murmuring, I'm here, it's only a dream. I gulp air and hold it in my lungs, willing a slowed pace of heartbeat, and eventually I lie down, curving my body into Edmund's. His hand drapes over my hip, sliding along my stomach to my waist, pulling me closer, the warmth of his body flowing into me. I concentrate on the rhythm of his breath, which slips over my collar at the back of my neck, feeling myself drawn inwards, downwards, sleepwards. Again I find myself in that room approaching the bed upon which Edmund lies. Again and again I start from the dream, which remains the same, only the body on the bed grows more desiccated, more decayed, until finally all that bleeds upon my touch is a skull bleached white as if by the sun.

ii

She was a beauty, Frances Howard, there is no denying it. Tiny face, delicate features, golden hair. On the day that Edmund and I visited Audley End, I had stood and gazed at her portrait, the daughter of the house. Lady Frances Howard, later to be the Countess of Sussex and later still the Countess of Somerset. I had heard of her before purchasing the collection of books on women criminals, how could one have not. All the major writers of her day had written about her, celebrating her marriages: Ben Jonson, Francis Bacon, Thomas Campion, John Donne. I studied her beauty and understood why. Of course,

Edmund had muttered, the painting was exaggerated, an idealization. I didn't care. My eyes had lingered over her milky skin, the rosebud mouth, the elaborate ruff that concealed her neck, the stiff fabric of the costume that encased her body, yet opened to reveal her breasts and only just covering the tips of her nipples.

Edmund had told me that she was a poisoner, banished from the court of James I for her role in the murder of the courtier Sir Thomas Overbury. Now, as I sat in the bookshop I hungrily read the story again, craving the details. To hold a book in my hand induces symptoms akin to kleptomania. A driving need to possess, to have, to take, that is assuagable only in opening the book, eyes grabbing words to squirrel them away in my head.

My mind absorbed the words of her life, but the more I read the less I wished to. For all these books that claimed to be about Frances Howard were about everything but *her*, or her role in the poisoning of Overbury. These books strained to absolve her of her actions, telling instead the history tales of famous men, documenting their activities while relegating Frances's connivances to the periphery. These books were not about Frances Howard at all.

Frances, who had plotted the imprisonment of her enemy Overbury because he was a threat to the annulment of her marriage, knowing, as he did, of her affair with Robert Carr, the king's favourite. Then, once Overbury had been incarcerated in the Tower of London, Frances had proceeded to poison him, supplying tarts powdered with white arsenic instead of sugar, partridges dressed in a sauce in which cantharides was used instead of pepper. Cantharides, a powder made from the dried wings and body of a beetle native to southern Spain and

Italy, an irritant, it causes nausea, vomiting, colic, bloody diarrhoea and urine. All symptoms which Overbury suffered. Yet he remained unsuspecting of the food served to him, for Jacobean food was richer than ours is, more highly sauced and flavoured, ideal, as Frances knew, for the masking of poison.

It took six months for Overbury to die and was finally achieved when Frances intercepts a clyster – what today we would call an enema – that has been prescribed for Overbury's undiagnosed illness. Within hours of the administration of the clyster, which contains sublimate of mercury, Overbury dies in great agony. Two months later Frances marries her lover Robert Carr, the Earl of Somerset.

But her happiness is short-lived and it is only two years before Frances is brought to trial. Four others, who assisted her in obtaining Overbury's death, have already been found guilty and hanged. Both Frances and Carr, who has also been implicated in the poisoning, plead guilty, are found guilty and given the death sentence. The sentence, however, is not implemented and the couple are imprisoned in the Tower of London for the next six years. Upon release they are banished from court. In 1633, at the age of thirty-nine, Frances dies from a uterine disorder, possibly cancer, an agony that her contemporaries gleefully liken to that of being poisoned, and is buried in the parish church of Saffron Walden.

Many at the court of James I had had their own reasons for wanting Overbury dead, but it is not possible to deny Frances's role in the poisoning, despite the attempts of innumerable authors to do so. A surfeit of books telling so little of her, relegating her role to that of the innocent pawn of powerful men. Standing up, I walk to the window and watch the rain fall in torrents. Through this shroud I look into the other bookshops, all brightly lit as if a stage, with the booksellers waiting for the curtain of rain to lift allowing the performance to begin.

iii

We sit and drink tea together, Edmund and I. I have coaxed him out of the bookshop to avoid being alone with him. A short time after his arrival this morning he startled me by talking about an eyedropper. What had he thought of my blank incomprehension as I asserted that I did not possess an eyedropper? How then could he have found one on my kitchen bench-top, he asked? Was it just bemusement on his face as I back-pedalled saying, oh *that* eyedropper, well, I use it for eardrops, which is probably why I don't think of it as an eyedropper. Perhaps I had been too vehement in my denial. Had I fooled him with the nonchalance with which I reached into the cupboard to take the eyedropper down from where he had placed it, moving it conspicuously to the window ledge?

I hadn't even noticed its absence. How I would have panicked this Thursday if I had been unable to locate the eyedropper to measure out the poison for Edmund's tea. Only then would I have realized that he must have seen it when tidying the kitchen and moved it, or thrown it out. I would hardly have been able to ask: Edmund, where have you put the eyedropper which I have been using to measure poison into your tea for the past, how many weeks? How many weeks has it been? Six? Five?

As he leant against the door jamb watching my face, I suggested we go out and wander around art galleries instead of going for a drive into the country as we had planned. He was irritable about the change in plan but I did not want to be alone with him. I wanted the distractions of other people, required the sense of being on show, unprivate in a public space, maintaining a social facade. The art, well, the art would give us a topic of conversation, a distraction from an eyedropper containing poison. How easy it would be to come unstuck, to watch the veneer behind which I have been hiding my murderous activities lift to peel away like cheap wallpaper and reveal the original foetid state of the wall beneath.

So we sit in a café drinking tea, trying to decide what art exhibition to go to. Edmund was leaving the decision to me, so that if he didn't like the exhibition he could blame it on my choice. I felt unable to choose, felt spoilt for choice. Death it seemed was the fashion of the moment. Ancient Egyptian Mummy portraits. Seventeenth-century anatomical figures sculpted in wax – female forms laid out on tables with heads thrown back, lips parted in orgasmic delight while their sliced-open stomachs revealed glistening intestines and wombs. Late nineteenth-century photographs of the death masks of literary greats. Photographs of ordinary men, women and children laid out in their caskets, babies in their mothers' arms as if asleep, as fascinating for their depiction of burial costume as for the expressions on the faces of the deceased. And so on and so forth. I read to Edmund the quotes describing each exhibition in the gallery guide. Occasionally Edmund spits into a tissue the excess spittle that clogs his mouth and wipes his right eye, which brims with water, yet spills over and rolls down his cheek. He is apologetic, disgusted at his body's weakness, but I am able to remain unperturbed, calm in the knowledge that it is my poison producing his symptoms.

We are silent together, Edmund looking out of the window, me mulling over the exhibitions list. Then he says, I know. Know what? I ask without looking up. I know what you're doing, he says. My eyes adhere to the words on the page. So, he knew. How long had he known? I resisted the urge to stand up and run, to flee, to say: so prove it, to say: don't be ridiculous. Instead I begin to cry, hiding behind one hand, shielding my distorted face from his sight. I lift my head towards the window as if looking out at the crowds hidden beneath umbrellas while he tells me what he knows. He knows, he says, that he is dying. He knows that I am trying to evade this fact by avoiding being alone with him. But he needs to talk about his death and takes my free hand before beginning to speak pragmatically of the decisions he is making and taking, given the fact that he believes that he is dying. I cry harder, as I realize that he doesn't know what I am doing after all. My body jolts as I bawl open-mouthed, feeling warm snot trickle to the edge of my nostrils prior to a further downwards slide onto my lips. Eventually I run out of tears and sit there snivelling and sniffing, staring at my reflection in the window.

I want to go home. My head throbs, I feel queasy, but Edmund, having found relief in his interpretation of my distress, wants to go on to an exhibition. In the street we huddle together beneath his umbrella and have hardly taken a dozen steps before I stop and lean into the gutter to heave the contents of my pot of tea. Solicitously Edmund holds the umbrella over me and as I straighten he gently wipes my mouth with a tissue. My discomfiture is evident, for as he dabs my mouth as if I were a child, he tells me that it is all right, he has grown rather used to vomit in the recent weeks. He places his arm around my shoulder as we continue to walk along, holding me close to his side so that it seems the most natural gesture in the world for me to reciprocate by placing my arm around his waist.

Inside the gallery we disengage to wander the rooms alone. Edmund has chosen contemporary work, despite professing to loathe recent art. He calls its current acceptance the elevation and triumph of the banal. The exhibition we are viewing is a collection of photographs in which the artists expressed their responses to, and sensibility of, the world of sudden death. The first room is installed with photographs of ordinary streets from faceless towns and suburbs – houses, gardens, footpaths, cars – all devoid of people. The world we encounter daily as still life. The accompanying text, which I read before stepping back to resume my inquisitive study of the photograph, told of some horrific act that had taken place on that street, in that house, in that garden, on that footpath. The ordinariness of each place, the lack of some stain remaining as a trace of the crime that had occurred, was meant to assault the viewer, as there were no hints nor clues to the grisly deaths these places had absorbed. These photographs display the easy resumption of normality.

The walls of the following room are hung with the photographs of murdered women. Re-photographed photographs that had appeared in the newspapers at the time of death. A snapshot portrait from each decade of the century, black and white, six foot by six, with, in front of each, set up on a plinth, as if on an altar, a woman's handbag with its contents strewn around it. All those things that women carry in their purses. Yet the artist has not just filled any old purse with any old clutter and placed it on the plinth; she has worked from archival forensic photographs that show each woman's dead body with her purse, sometimes still clutched in her hand, more often than not quite close to her body. The artist had then spent months scouring vintage women's magazines in order to find out just what the lipstick tube, or comb, or deodorant, or perfume, or sanitary napkin would be like that the women would carry given their time and place in our century. She had then made replicas of these items and placed them in hand-made replica bags, before turning them upside down and opening the clip or catch or zip to dump the contents onto the floor. Then she had photographed the placement of each fallen item and reproduced the layout on top of the plinth in front of the photograph. To my eye it seemed easy, but this room contained nearly three years' work. I was not sure what it told me about death, but I found it absorbing, intriguing. What was implied about the life of each woman from the items that she carried in her bag at the time of her death? Was I meant to see a link, see a particular item as a sign, an intimation of an impending cessation of life? I felt so, but was unable to make the connections.

The third and final room contains photographs of a doll's house that the artist herself had constructed with immense delicacy. As I looked at these intricate photographs I dwelt upon the finicky nature of building a doll's house with such exceptional exactness and was three-quarters of the way around the room before I was struck by what I was being shown. I went back to the beginning. In the living room a spray of blood trailed mesmerizingly up the tiny wall and along the ceiling. In the bathroom blood-stained clothes lay in a heap. In the kitchen a bloodied knife, and in the sink something spongy and white was clogging the minuscule sink-hole. And on the floor of the kitchen three fingers had fallen. Black bin-liners ranged near the back door awaited removal to a car in the garage that would take them away. In an ante-room to the room of photographs stood the doll's house itself, set on the floor, with the back wall missing, so that I could crouch down and look in to view the original tiny rooms and pieces of furniture that had then been photographed.

I wander back to the first room looking for Edmund, looking again at the photographs, finding them on second viewing slightly trite, somewhat obvious. These artists, by focusing on the absent, the not-there, insist that the viewer merge with the victim, become passive and inert. But where then does that leave the aggressor, the perpetrator of the crime? Still hidden, still faceless, waiting out of sight, somewhere, for someone.

iv

I recognized the name immediately: Offément, near Compiègne. Edmund and I had picnicked there, had followed the long drive that had been signposted Offément, then pulled the car off into the woods, stopping under a tree in full view of the chateau to eat bread and cheese, and drink red wine. It had been after our visit to Paris, my first trip to Paris. We had rented a car to venture into the countryside, enabling us to explore the beech and oak forests of Compiègne, the banks of the Oise and Aisne rivers. It had been so hot, such a hot July. I had fallen in love with Paris, with France. Perhaps, I had said to Edmund, I should have a bookshop in Paris. Leave London. He was horrified, although he was as enamoured of France as I was.

I sit in the bookshop transfixed with my remembered fantasies of a bookshop in the Rue de Lappe, or the Rue de la Roquette at the cemetery end. Is there anyone who does not love Paris? I became different when there, a glutton, gorging myself on whatever came my way, revelling in the spotlight of frequent Parisian glances. I laugh in memory of Edmund jealously saying that the only drawback to France was French men and their worshipful absorption in themselves. Frenchmen, according to Edmund, were not to be taken seriously by women, were merely there to be flirted with a little, then ignored.

Yes, I had been there with Edmund, Offément near Compiègne, where Marie-Madeleine d'Aubray had poisoned her father and two brothers. There were only a handful of books on her crimes and I decided to take them upstairs and look at them quietly, sip a glass of wine, preferably French, preferably red. Enough cataloguing for one day. I was tired, it had been a long day with people haggling over the prices, being in general boorish and vile. Some days, such as today, I loathed all humanity, would give up bookselling in a minute if there were anything else I could do. I settled myself with a tray of food, a bottle of wine, an open book upon my knees, shivering, toes curling in anticipation of the written word.

Marie-Madeleine d'Aubray, a Parisian, had been born into the French nobility in 1630 and was, from all accounts, cruel and wilful from her early childhood. She is described by her contemporaries as petite and graceful, with blue eyes and a mass of chestnut hair, retaining her looks until her death at the executioner's block at the age of forty-six, found guilty of three poisonings, while admitting to as many as fifty. At the age of twenty-one, she married the Marquis de Brinvilliers who shared her love of frivolity, yet it was not long before the Marquis and Marquise tired of each other and sought lovers.

Marie-Madeleine's lover was a cavalry officer and friend of her husband's named Gaudin Sainte-Croix, an inveterate gambler. With no sense of propriety they flaunt their relationship in public, Marie-Madeleine perhaps believing that if her husband was tolerant, which he was, so too would the rest of the world. She is greatly mistaken, for her father, a magistrate and state councillor for the city of Paris, took out a *Lettre de Cachet* against Sainte-Croix, ratified with the king's own seal, having him arrested and placed in the Bastille without trial.

Accounts vary as to how long Sainte-Croix remained in the Bastille, some say as little as six weeks, others three months. What is known is that at this time Marie-Madeleine begins to nurse a burning hatred of her father for this humiliation and begins to plot his death. If this seems a somewhat strong reaction to a situation that was caused by her own lack of discretion, the more prosaic fact is that she is deeply in debt, and requires money to cover both her own and Sainte-Croix's gambling losses, and on her father's death she is due to inherit a portion of his estate.

With Sainte-Croix's release from prison their relationship continues, albeit with more discretion, as does her plot to poison her father. In the Bastille, Sainte-Croix has come into contact with a master poisoner called Exili who had provided him with a variety of tips for the use of poison, the most useful of which was that arsenic could be purchased at the pharmacy of the king's apothecary. But Marie-Madeleine was not rash. Even if she did appear shallow and vacuous she was also clever and scheming. She sets out to test the effects of variable quantities of poison on the patients of the Hôtel-Dieu, the public hospital, near where she lived. Naïvely, her father is delighted, pleased that his daughter is assuming responsibilities suitable to her position in society by doing charitable works. She becomes a familiar figure at the Hôtel-Dieu, always bringing with her food for the patients. That those who become the object of her attention die in immense agony within twenty-four hours of her visit is said to cause her terrible sadness.

By the summer of 1666 she was practised enough to poison her father. Already ill he has retired to the family estate of Offémont. Marie-Madeleine devotes herself to nursing him. Inevitably under her ministrations he grows no better. In her later confession she will admit to dosing his food with poison at least twenty-eight times and will be quoted as saying that he had taken so long in dying that she thought he would never get to the end of it. After his death, to allay the rumours that arise that her father has been poisoned, Marie-Madeleine cannily insists on an autopsy being performed which finds his death due to natural causes.

Within three years she has frittered away her inheritance through her continued support of Sainte-Croix as well as through liaisons with additional lovers. By 1670 she is involved in attempts to poison her two brothers in order to obtain their share of the estate, and within four months of each other they too have succumbed. Rumours of poisoning resurface, fuelled by her brothers' widows. Once more she insists on autopsies. It seems that in France at this time the effects of arsenic poisoning were not identifiable. Instead, upon finding exactly the same damage to the internal organs in both brothers to that of their father, the surgeons attribute their deaths to an obscure hereditary illness. Marie-Madeleine's husband, however, seems to be in no doubt as to what his wife is doing; Brinvilliers flees to his own country estate where he employs a manservant to taste his food to safeguard his own health.

Marie-Madeleine had, however, been careless during the poisonings of her two brothers. Her arrogance led her to lower her guard, with the result that the valet to one of her brothers, as well as the tutor to her children, had become aware of her activities. She had gloated to the tutor over her conduct and used her brother's valet as her accomplice in administering the poison. In addition Sainte-Croix is now heavily blackmailing her. He has thirty-four incriminating letters from her in which she has outlined her plans for poisoning her family. These he keeps locked in a red casket alongside phials of poison. Marie-Madeleine's response is to attempt to have him murdered too. When unsuccessful, she threatens to poison herself if he does not destroy the letters and indeed takes arsenic, but administers herself an antidote immediately by drinking copious quantities of hot milk.

When, in 1672, Sainte-Croix is found dead in the small laboratory attached to his home in which he dabbled in alchemy and the mixing of poisons, Marie-Madeleine was for once not involved. Sainte-Croix, it seems, had accidently poisoned himself. Marie-Madeleine's prime concern becomes the obtaining of the red casket, but unfortunately for her this is already in the hands of the police. The valet is the first to be questioned. Initially he keeps his cool, but upon being informed that the casket has been opened and the letters read, he attempts to flee. He is tortured and at first reveals nothing of the poisonings, but just as he is about to die, he confesses to his role in his master's death and further to Marie-Madeleine's complicity. Marie-Madeleine flees, being sentenced *in absentia* to death by beheading. For the following three years she goes into hiding, fleeing to London, then moving on to Cambrai, Valenciennes, Antwerp and Liège where, having taken refuge in a nunnery, she is finally arrested in March 1676. If she had ever hoped for leniency due to her high-born position this ends when a written confession is found in the room that she occupies. In her own handwriting she confesses not only to the murders of her father and brothers but also to those of the patients of the Hôtel-Dieu, with further attempts on the lives of her sister, her daughter and a number of maidservants, none of which were successful.

Tried over a period of four months in twenty-two sittings, she never loses her spirit. Denying everything, she states that she had written the confession when ill and feverish, insisting that the letters had been forged by Sainte-Croix. Even in the face of the tutor's damning testimony she remains insolent and contemptuous. Ultimately, however, she is condemned, sentenced to be tortured by water, to public penance in front of Notre-Dame, and then beheading, her body to be burnt and her ashes scattered.

The only likeness of Marie-Madeleine known to exist is a sketch by Charles LeBrun of her crouched in a cart being transported to her execution. Unflattering, it shows her dressed in the white shirt worn by criminals, face horror-stricken and contorted. On the platform on which she would be beheaded, it is said that she sat quietly for the half hour it took for the executioner to cut her hair, so thick was it. My hand brushes the back of my own neck imagining the tug of shears slicing at hair, cold metal irregularly hitting the nape of the neck. Once her neck had been cleared of protecting hair, Marie-

165

Madeleine's eyes were bandaged, and at eight in the evening, in front of the crowds who had flocked to witness her execution, her head was severed with one stroke of the axe.

v

I awake to sunshine. Through the window I can see the intense blue of the sky. Thursday again. I curl onto my side. Through my closed eyelids the light penetrates making my eyeballs ache. Sunlight is such a rarity during the English winter. This afternoon Edmund shall visit me. We shall take tea together as we have done over the past decade, as we have done over the past six weeks. I have decided that I must poison him and have done with it. The question is, today or next week? Today? Why not today? Why put it off until next week? I turn onto my other side, away from the sunlight, and swing my legs off the side of the bed and sit up. Choosing my clothes with care, I dress.

Nearer four o'clock the sky has clouded to such a dirty white that it feels as if a piece of grimy muslin has been draped between myself and the world, blurring the edges, smothering contact. I sit on my hands and stare at the fire as I await Edmund. All is prepared. I have pierced the berries I have gathered from the privet hedge, in order to squeeze out and collect, in a teaspoon, their poisonous juices.

As he arrives he stops to look in the window as he has always done, then enters and I get up to shake his hand. His grip is still strong, it is one of the first things I noticed about him, the strength of his handshake. Firm hand, long fingers. The type to feel on one's body, brushing along one's skin, those fingers. We sit. We talk. I study his face which has been aged by his illness. There are lines under his eyes, dark circles, between his brows is a furrow, he would have made an elegantly handsome old man. Occasionally we catch each other's glance and hold the look, his brown eyes contemplating my green eyes. In this contact our complicity in the knowledge of his death is manifest.

I stand up to aid a customer who cannot locate what he requires, which is of course right in front of him, but then it is true that sometimes one cannot see for looking. I turn to find Edmund watching me, my movements, my face, and I walk to his side and say, shall I make tea and he nods yes. As I walk past him I allow my thigh to brush his shoulder and he lifts his hand to take my hand as I pass, fingers momentarily pressing into mine.

Upstairs I put on the kettle and when I hear the telephone ring I move back near the staircase to listen in case Edmund needs me. R. Hare, I hear him say, yes, speaking. It is a call for Edmund, I begin to move back towards the kitchen, when he says loudly, forcefully, no. By the time I am halfway down the stairs he has left the shop. On the street he is walking briskly away and I shout after him, knowing that my customers are staring avidly through the bookshop window. Edmund wait, I shout and start to run after him. Hearing my footsteps he begins to run from me, and so I stop.

Back in the bookshop my customers are suddenly reserved, the epitome of English discretion, slowly drifting out of the door without making a purchase, until I am alone. Upstairs the kettle whistles and I take the stairs two at a time to end its shrillness, fingers wrenching at the gas knob. I can't believe that he has gone, just like that. I veer between worry and fury the more I think of it. The best-laid plans, Mary always said. My hand finds the teapot and throws it. The wall flings back smashed fragments. But that is not salve enough. Thereafter I pace, waiting for his phone call, and as the hour grows later I move onto the sofa, hugging my legs to my chest, rocking a little, sitting in the dark, waiting for his call. Bastard. Of all the days. How could he leave without a word. How dare he. The best-laid plans, Mary always said.

During my first year at the bookshop it could hardly be said that I had a plan of action. A routine yes, a strategy no. I would get up in the morning and go down to the bookshop and do the tasks that needed to be done. Eventually this became the structure around which my life was based. That it was successful is, I think, pure luck. In that first year all those people who were to become my regulars came in, some wandering in out of curiosity, others on a mission, some delighted at its metamorphosis, others furious. As the months passed I learnt their likes and dislikes, developed an ability to preempt their requests and requirements. It was strangely exhausting work, who would have thought it of bookselling, but it was a day-long performance, one's manners and mannerisms having to change according to the person being dealt with. Within six months I had shortened my opening times from six days a week to three, in order to go out on buying trips to refill the gaps on my shelves. Even on my quiet days I did not lack tasks: responding to mail requests, tidying the shelves, answering the telephone. I had bought a computer to enable me to catalogue my stock, and after much bungling finally had it running in a fashion that I could decipher.

I drew attention by my window displays, which I changed once a week. Whether I wanted to or not, I did it. I focused on obituaries, bought myself a calendar of literary dates and events and plundered it. Not a very good book, it did, however, have a number of deaths for every date. Once a week I would pick a name whose anniversary of their death fell during the forthcoming week, preferably someone of whose books I had copies, and then I would do a memorial window. I would locate an old jacket photograph, enlarge it on the photocopier I kept in the basement, put it in a frame, then in the window, surrounded with the author's books. Even better was when a living author died, then I would redo the window, a framed obituary from the paper, a bunch of flowers, and a casual stack of books, in some cases only one or two. My windows were appreciated, not only by my regulars. On occasion I have had people ask if they might also leave a flower in the window, or some small token such as a scribbled message on a folded piece of paper. But this is rare, it has only happened on three occasions, the most recent one was the death of Edmond Jabès.

A writer's death. It is a fallacy that a writer's death means nothing to those who read of it in the newspaper. How it haunts the reader, the realization that never again will words form sentences under the guidance of a particular hand. The comprehension that yet again the reader is on his or her own to search out in that saturation of books a writer who has the power to instil the faith that one is not alone, that there are two of us, you know. I often think that to be touched by a writer's work is the most miraculous thing in the world, even better perhaps than being the writer.

But then how would I know, for although I write I am not a writer, for to be a writer is to be published, to have a book on a shelf that has one's name on the spine. During my first year at the bookshop I tried to become a writer. I sent my manuscript off to publishers who sent it back again. Twelve times in all. With no comment beyond, on two occasions, a no thank you typed on a compliments slip. But I would not be deterred. I started again, targeting writers' agents, only this time the letters that came back with my manuscript were longer. Two-page letters telling me everything that was wrong with my story, my structure. In some cases I knew that the reader had not gone beyond page five or six, for these letters, still saying no thank you, were not talking about my manuscript at all.

So I gave up and started again, another novel that is, and was halfway through it on the day that Edmund first came to the bookshop. Of course I knew who he was, I like to think that it wasn't because of who he was that I was nice to him. I'm sure I didn't think, now here's someone who might help me get my book published, I wasn't like that then, I was still too Australian, too straightforward, too plain-spoken. Now I will tell anyone whatever it is I think they want to hear, just so long as I get what I want from the transaction.

It was unseasonably warm for a day in early spring, the first time I met Edmund. I watched through the bookshop window as people suddenly seemed to discern the heaviness of their winter coats. I had opened the door and the window at the back, overlooking the courtyard that I was slowly filling with pots and creeping ivy to cover the walls. Once in a while, if the breeze moved in the right direction the sounds of the train station would leap the wall and meander through the window, past the sleeping forms of the cats who had adopted me. On my desk was a vase of jonquils, early, tender buds. I sat there filled with the joys of spring, sleeves pushed up past my elbows, tapping away at the keyboard, the smell — that is almost not a smell, so frail and precarious is it — of jonquil flirting with the hairs of my nostrils. I smiled: at the computer screen, at the books, at myself, at the world going past outside the window, at Edmund Maskelyne peering in through the window. I knew who he was, how could I not, I am a reader as well as a bookseller. I had read his recently published first novel which someone had brought into the shop to sell, a review copy, unread. It wasn't that I had disliked it. No, that would be too strong a word, but I did realize that it was not perhaps as good as it should be, or as the reviewers were saying it was. That perhaps if Edmund had not been a Maskelyne his novel might never have encountered printer's ink at all.

He came in and I was polite, not betraying the fact that I recognized him, and after a lengthy browse he bought a book, paying in cash, before leaving. He was handsome, that is what struck me, even now I can remember that, for I had encountered his face in the newspapers looking dour and sour, thin and awkward. In the flesh he seemed fuller, more broad of face. Slender yes, but not thin. Tall with dark brown hair falling, in that floppy English schoolboy way, into brown eyes. With the most beautiful hands I had ever seen: strong wrists opening into wide palms and long slender fingers with well-shaped trimmed fingernails. Strong, healthy hands, that curved the length of a pen, that turned the pages of books.

He came on Thursdays, sometimes not, but never any other day. His moods changed each week: liverish, shy, boorish, charming, pedantic, witty, needy, indifferent. On the days that he seemed keen to chat I would always be a bit too busy to engage with him, except for a few moments. Deliberately, of course, I was playing a game. I knew it. On Thursday mornings I paid slightly more attention to my appearance than I normally did. I wanted his attention. I hadn't got so far as to think that maybe I could use him to obtain an introduction useful for getting published. Or had I? My book, I remember thinking, was no worse than Edmund's book, I just needed some contacts. On one very hot summer's day he arrived just as I was locking the door to go upstairs to get a glass of iced tea. After explaining that no, I wasn't closing for the day, he offered to come in and watch the shop while I, as he described it, disappeared behind the beaded curtain to get the tea. I reappeared with a glass for him and he stayed and we chatted for an hour or so, and then the following Thursday he appeared just in time for tea. Or so I told him.

We encountered each other at book launches and signings. Unlike some of those who were content to chat to me in R. Hare but then in a social situation would behave as if they had never seen me before, Edmund would always chat and make sure that I was invited to move on to wherever everyone else was going as well. We shook hands when meeting and he called me Miss. I, for some obscure reason, studiously avoided the use of his name. We got drunk together many times and he would tell me about his family, Hermione in particular, after which I would bundle him into a taxi that would take him home. He assisted my entrée to the closed world of weekend literary events, pulling strings that would enable me to set up a stall of books. I was grateful, how could I not be, but it was not what I wanted. I wanted him to introduce me to a publisher. It was not that he was not interested in my writing, he was profoundly hostile. He loathed and feared anyone who wrote, even unsuccessfully, seeing them as competition, always better than he would ever be. In the rare moments that I would talk about my book, my writing, he would slowly disengage from the conversation, so that I was left talking to myself with little alternative but to change the subject.

He drove me to Suffolk to show me the house that he had lived in during the school holidays, took me to the parish church where Hermione was buried, showed me the kneelers that she had embroidered in between writing. Told me how she would sit with her embroidery at hand so that when she couldn't write, or would need to stop to think about a particular passage, she would pick up her embroidery. As we stood at her graveside people came to look at her grave, then chatted to Edmund, shaking the hand of Hermione's grandson, while I stood there ignored. Afterwards we drove to the sea and after too many pints of bitter went for a long walk. All the way Edmund talked of his family, his writing, himself. Sitting to look at the view we were silent. Then I said it must be the most awful bore being a Maskelyne, having the weight of Hermione's reputation grinding down his own wish to write. It was a half-truth, juxtaposed with the thought that he was an incredibly lucky bastard with his name and connections and that perhaps he should get on with his life and stop bloody whingeing.

But, I had, it seemed, said the right thing, for not long after that we became lovers and even after that went awry we continued to see each other, travelling together, more and more often. All the places I've been to with Edmund, now that is a book in itself. Perhaps that is the book I should write. As we travelled I began to take photographs, snapshots of Edmund. I have them still. Hundreds of them. Edmund here, there and everywhere. I am not in them, for I was always the photographer. That at least is something I was better at than Edmund. Sometimes I get them out after I've had too much wine, when I'm feeling slightly maudlin, and reminisce about all the places that we have been to together. We had fun, Edmund and I, more than our share of adventures.

SEVEN

The next morning Edmund still had not telephoned, but he no longer needed to for I read of her death in the newspaper. A notice on the front page and a longer obituary inside. I am shocked, feel my gut clench in resistance to the words flailing at me. I knew her. She had been one of my regular customers. Edmund's friend, Eliza Looker. The details of her death are sketchy, it had only occurred the previous morning. She had collapsed after leaving the London train at Penzance; her mother had been there; there would be an autopsy to determine the cause of death. The obituary is a bland litany of her books, her projects.

I am shocked at her death, but am I upset? Should I call Edmund? Instead, knowing that Edmund will appreciate my gesture, I do the window, cutting out the obituary, placing it in a clip frame, then in the window, with a pile of her books. I try to recall what she spoke of during her last visit to the bookshop nearly two months ago, what books she had purchased, but I cannot. I bought the newspaper each day, bemused at the appreciations that began to flow, for I had understood that most people found her generally disagreeable. Appraisals and reappraisals of her work, women writing about the meaning of the death of a young woman. The spillage of words had nothing to do with grief and mourning, even less to do with the woman I had met on many occasions over the years. This was writing by insiders for insiders, proof that the scriveners themselves knew the right people, were doing something of importance, just as it was presumed Eliza had been. I read the names attached to the articles, encountering those that I knew, people to whom Edmund had introduced me, who came to my bookshop, then snubbed me at parties. Those whom I had heard make vituperative comments about her, denigrate her work, but then be pleasant to her when face to face. She was, now safely dead, a genius. Pre-eminent in her field. A visionary. Her work containing auguries of her early tragic death. Futilely I searched for Edmund's name appended to an article, but respectfully he maintained his silence.

When he arrived on Thursday he glanced briefly in the window before coming into the bookshop, seeming a trifle sad but in control. He explained that last week after being told the news of her death he had refused to believe it and had gone to her house; taking the key from where he knew it was hidden he had let himself in, looking for her. Walking from room to room, touching her books, going into her darkroom for the first time, lifting her cameras in his hand, the lenses, feeling the weight. Then he had made himself a cup of tea and sat at the kitchen table and waited for her to come home, even though he had known she would not.

Will he write something, I enquire. No, he tells me, how do you encapsulate a life in five hundred words. To do so would imply distance, an ability to focus on a particular aspect of her character. I knew her too well, he says, standing near the fire, eyes unseeing. I suppose I will be next, death always happens in threes, does it not? Would he like a cup of tea, I ask. He says he isn't thirsty.

After he is gone I go and stand in my courtyard, light from the bookshop illuminating the area. My fingers brush the thick buds of jonquils and daffodils made heavier by the raindrops. They are early this year, it has been a mild winter, wet and dark. The daphne has already bloomed, clusters of three stalkless flowers on a leafless shrub. But I shall pluck no flowers from this bush to poison Edmund, for if Eliza's death has unstopped such an outpouring what would the death of Hermione Maskelyne's grandson provoke? He would be deified, his paltry novels elevated to the realms of literature. Edmund would be famous. That is not what I want. At least not yet. Upstairs I look at my preparations for tea, ready in expectation of Edmund's visit, sharply defined under electric light.

Edmund must not die, not like this, not yet. I light the gas and make myself a cup of tea and sit quietly to drink it.

ii

On the drive to Penzance for the funeral Edmund insists on a detour; there is a place he wants to show me, has wanted to show me for some time since my obsession had begun with my women criminals. *My* women criminals? I look at him in the rear-view mirror. He laughs, you are obsessed with them, it is all that you talk about. He asks me how many more books I have to catalogue, resting his arms along the back of the seat. I have placed him in the back of the station-wagon, laying the seat down, filling the back with blankets and pillows so that he can rest and sleep when he wants to.

As I begin to mention some of the lives still to be catalogued in the remaining thirty-two boxes of books in my basement, he suddenly tells me to park. We walk through sodden fields, shoes noisily slipping on wet grass as we climb the hill. Inkpen Hill. Edmund's breath rasps in his throat as we reach the summit to stand beside the replica of a gibbet that had stood here in 1676. Above us the clouds race desperate to catch each other, and looking up I shade my eyes from the sun that periodically thrusts through. Piercing light, rapidly eclipsed. Once, the bodies of criminals hung here swaying in chains, eyes, pecked clean by birds, sightlessly brooding over the view from one of the highest chalk hills in England. My hand grips rain-drenched wood and I turn to look at Edmund who is momentarily caught in the shadow of the gibbet in a sudden flash of sunlight, his face paste-white, red smudges colouring high his cheekbones. I take his hands in mine, which retain the dampness of the gibbet, and raise them to my cheeks moulding his hands to my face. I won't let you die, I tell him. His eyes are like spotlights raking first one eye then the other, to and fro, searching. I smile, my cheeks swelling into his palms, I won't let you die, Edmund.

The walk down the hill is easier and at the car I turn and look back to the gibbet, silently speculating on how far the rancidness of a rotting body would have carried on a fine day.

Near Marazion it begins to snow, fat flakes slapping onto the windscreen, knocking into the daffodil heads, bright in the village window boxes. As I drive into Penzance, Edmund lifts his head to watch as we pass the train station, staring intently at the trainless track and sparsely populated platform wondering, I'm sure, where it is that Eliza fell. At our hotel on the seafront I sit by the window while he goes off to see her parents. Book open on my lap, whisky tumbler in my hand, I ruminate on the sea heaving thickly, swelling to lift then pause before dropping to smash onto the promenade. I watch the flakes falling neither fast nor slow, but in the certitude that at ground level they will form a covering for the earth. The incongruity of sea and snow. The utter ridiculousness of it all.

The following morning we awake to an eerie, resonant silence. Death, I say to Edmund, is white not black. I look out at an asphyxiated world, at a serene sea, at stalactites hanging from the railings of the promenade, glinting enticingly. Briefly there is a debate as to whether the funeral can proceed, for roads have been blocked. But her parents insist that the road be cleared, allowing the hearse to get through to the chapel, a raggle-taggle stream of cars trailing, one behind the other, engines stalling in the bitter cold. We disembark to walk the long winding path to the chapel, shoes crunching on the icy earth. Breath, warmed in lungs, expelled to smokily hover around lips.

To enter the chapel doors and be enveloped by the heat of hundreds of burning candles, eyes stinging from the heavy weight of incense, is a relief. I follow Edmund down the aisle and am introduced to Eliza's parents before we take a seat. In front of me the coffin is open, not lying flat on a bier as it should be but propped at an angle so that Eliza's face hovers in the candlelight. The movement of the flames casts shadows across her face, warming the pallor of her skin, softening the outlines so that at times it seems as if there is the slightest lifting of her lips, as if she is smiling, as if in amusement. Her father moves towards the coffin sliding his arm under her shoulders to lift her forwards, just a little. With his free hand he pulls her hair to one side from where it lies beneath her head, before he gently places her head back on the pillow. His fingers sift through her thick chestnut hair arranging the long waves so that they fan her face on one side and tumble down her chest. My throat tightens as he turns to us who softly watch and tells us that she has always hated lying on her hair, that she prefers it to one side when she sleeps. Then he sits down beside Eliza's mother.

Intermittently throughout the service I could hear the sound of crying. Edmund focused on the hymnal, voicelessly mouthing the words. Briefly I studied her parents, she slight and dark, he tall and golden, both inward, untear-stained. I study her face, Eliza's face, as I had never been able to in life. To look at her had been like throwing an object at a wall and expecting it to stick, when all it could achieve was a useless downwards descent. In the absence of her scrutiny I study her. She had been a beauty from the left side but not from her right, in life she had vaguely resembled a Millais reworked by Picasso, if that is possible. That heavy pallid skin, the reams of chestnut hair, then the lopsided face, one eye smaller, lower than the other, heavily lidded so that it often seemed half closed, while the other eye watched, obelisk-like. Oddly this irregularity is not noticeable with her eyes closed, in sleep, in death. She is dressed in the black suit she always seemed to wear, buttoned tightly around her neck, and I wonder at the damage hidden beneath that the coroner had wrought when opening her body, rummaging to find her cause of death. An accidental death, Edmund had told me. An accident. Meaning what, I had asked. Meaning, what a fucking waste, he had said, not angrily, but in the tone of voice in which one said, it's raining, or, would you like another cup of tea.

As the service ended and the coffin lid was lowered I looked at her for the last time. Was it a panacea to think that she looked restful, peaceful, at ease? What would she say, what would she think, if she knew that her death had provided a reprieve from death for Edmund? That by dying she had saved him, temporarily. As Edmund stands to take his place beside her father and the four others who are to carry her coffin, my mouth twists and I clench my jaw to still the trembling of my lips. It has always been a sight that affects me, that of a black box borne upon the shoulders of a gathered group of men. There is something primeval in such a sight, a timeless action. As I stand to follow, I stumble, feet frozen from the cold, but by shuffling I can move and feel the agonizing circulation of blood resume in my feet.

Outside a blue sky blazes overhead, sunlight ruthlessly reflected on white snow, the blue sea depthless in the distance. Blue and white, brutally juxtaposed, the gash of earth vibrantly interjecting, life affirming against their frigid tones. As the coffin is lowered into its depths her mother lifts her head away to look to the horizon while her father presses his hands against his mouth forcing his anguish to remain internal. In deference to their despair I look away, eyes desperate for a focus, fixing on the daffodils clustered around headstones, green stemmed, yellow nozzled, some bent under the weight of snow, some flattened, some unyielding, persisting valiantly in an upright position.

iii

At the hotel we drink whisky, relaxing, succumbing to the warmth. We had stayed only briefly at the gathering at her parents' house. Edmund couldn't bear it, the nuns, the sepulchral tones, as if Eliza had died, he said.

What then does he think death is, I ask. He doesn't know, stumbles with words to tell me that no one ever dies

183

because as long as someone is alive who remembers the deceased then that person continues to live. For example, as long as he lives Eliza will live, for he had known her and will carry her memory with him. What happens, I ask, when there is no one left to remember? That is why we have to talk about the dead, he says, so that even people who never knew Eliza will know her and her memory will be passed on to them, and then they will pass on that memory to others, and so on and so on. But that is not life, I tell him, that is the recollection of a life, the history of a life. Of course, he agrees, but life as it occurs is little more than the recollection of life. As I sit here and speak, what I say is already moving into the past. You are listening to me, but in order to respond you will need to recollect what I have said. Then you will interpret my words in a way that has very little to do with me but which has solely to do with you.

Let me clarify this, I say. You are telling me that when you die, that for as long as I am alive you are alive, as alive as you are now? Yes, he nods. Because, I say, in reality you are not alive for me even now, you are a series of actions and gestures and mannerisms for which I construct a meaning but which I will never understand because I cannot know your interior motive. So there is your life and then the story of your life according to whomever receives the image of your bodily person. But in addition you are saying that if I talk about you with people who may never have met you, then you will still continue to exist because they will carry some impression of you, no matter how fragmentary. So, in fact, we all live for ever. There is no such thing as death.

No, no, he says. We only begin to live when we are dead, only when we are no longer a physical presence are we alive. I ask: what then are you saying about us as physical presences now in this room? I am saying, Edmund says, that now that Eliza is dead, for me she will be truly alive, for there will not be an actual Eliza getting in the way of who and what I want her to be. Just as when I die I shall truly exist for you and if you died you would truly exist for me. We can only know someone in, by and through their absence. We can only construct a complete picture of someone after they are dead, when their contradictions are no longer apparent and obvious. But, I say, if it is a picture that is not based on an individual's complexity how then can it be a valid picture? The only person, he tells me, to whom one is valid is oneself. We can never know the intricacies of another and do not want to know the intricacies. In others we are solely looking for a reflection of ourselves, a confirmation of our own presence, which we will never find.

Why then are people friends, I ask. They're not, he tells me. We all hate each other, we are all enemies. So-called friendship is an attempt to pacify and tame the difference of the other person. We search for the points of similarity in order to repress our animal instinct which urges us to kill what we don't know and therefore fear. Secretly, he says, we all want each other dead so that then, and only then, we can allow each other to live.

Surprised by his vehemence, I argue the opposite, neglecting to disclose that, in fact, I am in agreement with every word he says.

iv

We stand at the hotel window looking up towards the chapel, where Eliza lies. Where Eliza's dead body will

185

disintegrate and crumble, while she will remain alive within us according to our needs, our whims, our fancies. A duplicity of Eliza's. Edmund's. Mine. We stand, our hands in the pockets of winter coats, snow melting from our boots to form ice-flecked puddles on the carpet. We have been out to buy another bottle of whisky, which we had opened in the street, swigging from it as we walked along, legs sinking knee-high into snowdrifts. We look at each other, sadly, drunkenly knowing that there is nothing to know. Edmund's cold fingers touch my face, the same fingers that have touched Eliza's face in her coffin. Are his fingers still carrying the coldness of her skin? His eyes look sightlessly into mine. What is it he sees? Eliza? Or his own face reflected in my pupils. I allow my eyelids to drop, returning me to myself, while his fingertips examine the grooves and hollows of my face.

He removes my coat, then his own, and comes to stand behind me, resting his chin on my shoulder, turning his face into my neck. I draw in the smell of whisky from his breath as he undresses me down to my knickers. The cold air emanating from the window hurts my skin and his cold hands on my stomach cause my nipples to harden. Unbuttoning his flies he rubs against me, hands stroking my back, around my hips. I make no attempt to touch him, my hands remain limply at my sides. When he is hard enough pressing into my back I slide my knickers down, bending slightly at the knees to lean forward, pushing my behind up into the air and tilting my spine forward, stretching to fold my arms on the window ledge, resting my forehead on my hands. Roughly he enters me so that the crown of my head bangs into the glass of the window and my fingers tighten around the cotton of my knickers which I still hold. I lower my face into their softness, nose nuzzling, seeking out my own smell which causes my mouth to fill with saliva. The tightness between my legs expands with each thrust of Edmund's, much as if a piece of thread was being pulled more and more tautly until it snaps to unravel and I am splitting apart, coming undone, so that my back arches and head lifts and I can hear a voice that I recognize as my own, dolorous, lamenting, Edmund, help me, help me.

I dream of death, my death, by drowning. In my dream I walk on sand, and as I walk towards the horizon, the sand which undulates endlessly laps at my feet to rise and tower over me in a wave whose spray sprinkles my face. I watch as the wave tumbles towards me and as it strikes my face I open my mouth and feel water fill my mouth and pour down my throat, its coldness seeping throughout the cavities of my chest, filling my lungs to such a capacity that the water that has poured in through my gaping mouth is forced upwards to gush out of my nostrils. All the while that this is happening my eyes remain open, fixed upon that endless wave tumbling into my mouth, until I realize that, in fact, I am dead. I have drowned.

The first time I had this dream I was three or four years old at the most, sleeping in the front of the van with Mary and Mackie asleep in the back. My eyes snapped open, expecting the gum trees I could see towering through the windscreen to tumble down upon me. Fearful, I sat up unable to utter a sound, peering over the seat to make sure that Mary and Mackie were still there, allowing the sound of their breathing to lull my shivering life. I must have fallen asleep for the next thing I knew the van was full of sunlight and I shook Mary awake because I needed to pee. Sleepily she carried me from the van, hooking her fingers in the elastic to slide my knickers down then holding me in the squatting position. She held me between her spread legs, my back curved into her belly, her hands tightly gripping my thighs, fingers pressing strongly to leave an imprint, her cheek against mine as we watched the yellow trickle fall to the ground, to be rapidly absorbed in the dusty earth. When I had finished she swung me up into her arms and carried me back to the van where I was allowed to nestle down beside her, where I would lie securely inhaling the slightly oily smell of her hair, for it was still long then, before she cut it short convinced that it made her look younger. I could feel the rough wool of her cardigan clenched in my hand and the brush of blanket against my chin as I drowsed while Mackie stoked the embers of the previous night's fire in order to boil water for tea, then passing a steaming cup through to Mary who would lean on her elbow to drink, blowing on it to cool the liquid before holding the cup to my lips.

On the day that the police came to the bookshop to tell me of Edmund's death, I sat daydreaming, eyes unfocused on the steam that wafted from my tea to dampen my face, lost in thoughts of Mary. Mrs Maskelyne? one policeman had asked. Yes? I had smiled. It was not unusual for the police to come in to browse when passing, but I did not know these two officers who now held their caps under their arms. Mrs Maskelyne, I'm afraid we have bad news. I stood to be on their level, my fingertips lightly touching the surface of my desk and said that perhaps we should go upstairs to be more private. I knew what they had come to tell me. I called Richard down from where he sat on the second floor, which was now no longer my sitting room but another room of the bookshop. On the third floor, my former bedroom, we sat, and they proceeded to tell me about Edmund's death.

How did they expect me to respond, those two officers who had encountered so many different reactions to grief, such a variety of forms of distress? What did they expect? The room was silent after they had finished speaking, although I could feel the laughter scratching at my throat. I tried to mask my sniggering but it edged around my hand to engulf the room, louder and louder, until my swollen stomach dully ached and I clasped my hands around it so as to ease the pain. It's my fault, I said, I killed him. But they would not listen, they persisted in reassuring me that it had been an accident.

A long time passed before they left, finally assured that I was not hysterical, nor a danger to myself or likely to go into premature labour. They made more tea, offered to drive me home, asked if there was someone they should telephone to keep me company. And as they went through the motions of officialdom I sat there contemplating the fact that Edmund had died more through sheer accident than from my plotting and planning. I remembered only hours before listening to Edmund's detailed plans for a lunch of roast pork, potatoes, onions, and recalled neglecting to inform him that there were no onions. I had watched him stand and break open the plastic bag of daffodil bulbs that I had left in the kitchen, and remove four in the belief that they were onions, placing them alongside the potatoes that he would later cook. I had sat passively watching, saying nothing, feeling the child kick against my kidneys and shift its weight to bear down on my bladder. Then I had stood up, saying that I would not stay for lunch after all, for six months into the pregnancy I only did half-days at the bookshop, usually arriving there after lunch at home with Edmund. I kissed him on the mouth and he followed me to the door, walking down the garden path with me, watching, waving until I was no longer in sight and had turned the corner. I walked to the bookshop where I then sat awaiting a telephone call, or the arrival of the police come to tell me of Edmund's accidental death. He had only eaten one bulb, I was later told, had pushed the others to the side of his plate, not liking the taste, perhaps. Daffodil bulbs were often mistaken for onions, they told me, there were many such cases of similar poisonings. When he had started to be sick he had called for an ambulance, but had convulsed, choking on his own vomit before help arrived. His death was an accident, they said.

After the funeral I left the bookshop, eventually moving the child and myself to Paris. Time passes quickly, I walk the child to school and collect him at the end of the day. In between I write and deal with the correspondence concerning Edmund's estate. His star ascended, just as I had known it would after his death, just as I had guessed after watching what happened following the death of Eliza. It was after her death that I tenderly cultivated the idea of marriage, until Edmund finally proposed, believing it to be his own idea. I realized that I would be a fool if I did not position myself so as to capitalize on his death.

I miss him, it would be a lie to say otherwise. I miss him the most when I awake at night, for sometimes I dream of death, my death by drowning. I miss his hand, warm at the base of my spine, and his voice murmuring that it's only a dream. Then I'll get up and go downstairs to the desk that was Edmund's, the desk at which I write. For I am published now. That was my leverage. If the publishers wanted access to Edmund's journals and diaries, I reasoned, then my writing would need to be considered as well.

I write stories of deviant women, criminal women. When I had finished my cataloguing I was unable to part with the books, consumed with resentment at the thought of them on another's bookshelves. Now I rewrite the lives they contain, telling the tales of my women criminals, fictionalized to be more palatable. For even today the world does not want to be told that women are not as nice as perhaps they ought, or are thought, to be. On my desk is a photograph of Edmund and me, a rare one of us together, for I do not like being photographed. My face is always different, I never look the same. In this photograph we're laughing: an attractive couple, standing together. Edmund resembles Edmund, but I could be a stranger. That can't be me, I always think, when I look at it.

I call the child Max, although the name on his birth certificate is Edmund McCloskey Maskelyne. He loves me, this child, loves me like an animal, clambers on top of me and tumbles over me, is in perpetual need of physical contact. Even when I push him away it is not long before he is back, arms draped around me. I have told him that I was born Mary Miss McCloskey on December 27th, 1964 in outback New South Wales. I tell him of Mackie and Mackie's mother, of Mary and of Edmund. He listens avidly to my stories, fascinated by Australia, and keeps asking when we can go. Later, I say, when you are older.

We travel rarely, Max and I, we are content with our apartment on the Rue Charles V. From time to time we visit London. We'll go to the bookshop that Richard manages for me, for I've kept R. Hare for Max in case he is more drawn to bookselling than to writing. Those visits grow less and less frequent. They unsettle me, make me uneasy. I find myself looking towards the window as if I am waiting for Edmund to appear and to pause, before coming in and shaking my hand. Then I am swamped with longing for the infinitesimal variety of rainy days that England has to offer and I consider returning to London, to the bookshop. Until I turn and see Max, who looks so like Edmund that it causes my heart to expand and push against my ribs until they ache. I don't notice the resemblance when we are at home, but at the bookshop I see it, struck anew.

It is often after our trips to London that I am swept with the urge to cause Max pain, to crush him, to annihilate him. It is an urge that rushes at me like the wind, buffeting me with its sudden force so that I have to stand rigid in order not to shift under its strength. At these times I will send him from me, to his room, to his friends, and I will seat myself at Edmund's desk and force myself to write, fingers stabbing at the keyboard until the urge to destroy has subsided, alleviated by my writing.

It is when he is away from me that I love him the most, the wish for his company developing into yearning. Yet his return is always a disappointment to me and I will feel embarrassed by my need for him. At those times I am aware of how easy it would be to poison a child, so much easier than to poison a grown man. It would be too easy, almost.

Max has begun to keep a photograph of me on his desk, where he sits to do his homework, near the window from which he can see the buttresses of Notre-Dame. It was taken recently, accidentally, by myself. I can't remember what I was trying to photograph but the shutter clicked and the image that came out was of my shadow projected onto the earth. The moment Max saw it he wanted it for his desk, insisting that it could only be me. The outline of curly hair, the awkward stance, the shape of the lifted hand holding the camera, a shadow against the twigs and stones and earth. When I told Max that, truly, it could be anyone, his face took on that determined look, so typical of Edmund, that I consented. Then, lifting his head from studying the photograph, he smiled. When he smiles at me I know that I must never hurt him, that I must always resist my wish to hurt him, for he has Mary's smile, her mouth, her habit of gnawing the inside of her bottom lip with her teeth. My Mary. What would she think of Max, I wonder. No, I must never harm him. I could never harm him. Could I?

Sometimes my son dreams of my death, apparently it is a phase that all children go through, dreaming the death of their mother. Crying, he will climb into bed with me, needing to be reassured that I will never die, never leave him. But I will not lie to him, and have told him that it could happen, at which moment he will insist that when I die, he

192

will also. I hold him until his shivering ceases, burying my nose into his soft mass, curved into my body, and delight in his child's smell of soap and skin. I wonder if my odour soothes him likewise, for we do have our similarities Max and I, but he is going to be tall like his father. Soon he will be taller than me.

Acknowledgements

I would primarily like to thank Simon Morley, who first read the 'completed' manuscript, and whose eagle eye teased out many irregularities. Similar can be said of Laura Longrigg and Henry Sutton. I thank all three for their endless patience and support during the writing of this book. Thanks also to Ian Shipley who, with his booksellers, runs the best bookshop in London.

My thanks must also go to the librarians of the former North Library of The British Library, Bloomsbury, for their tireless assistance in locating the books that I required, some of which had been placed in storage for the move to St Pancras. The following books, to which I am indebted, should be read as a selected bibliography and are by no means a complete list of sources used.

Elizabeth Jeffries:
The Authentick Tryals of John Swan and Elizabeth Jeffryes (1752); *The Trial at Large of John Swan and Elizabeth Jeffries, Spinster, for the Murder of her Late Uncle* (1752)

Mary Blandy:
It is Margaret Anne Doody's observation, and not my own, that Mary's 'Own Account' shows the literary influence of Aphra Behn. This is to be found in Doody's fascinating essay 'The Law, the Page, and the Body of Woman. Murder and Murderesses in the Age of Johnson', published in *The Age of Johnson, A Scholarly Annual* (1987).

Miss Mary Blandy's Own Account of the Affair Between her and Mr Cranstoun from the Commencement of their Acquaintance in theYear 1746 to the Death of her Father in August 1751 (1752); *Memoirs of the Life of William Henry Cranstoun, Esq.* (1752); *The Secret History of Miss Blandy* (1752); *A Candid Appeal to the Publick Concerning the Case of the Late Miss Mary Blandy* (1752); *The Letters of Horace Walpole* (1891); *The Trial of Mary Blandy* by William Roughead (1914)

Mary Sayer:
A Full and Faithful Account of the Intrigue Between Mr Noble and Mrs Sayer (1713); *A Full Account of the Case of John Sayer, Esq.* (1713)

Margaret Caroline Rudd:
Mr Daniel Perreau's Narrative of His Unhappy Case (1775); *Facts, or a Plain and Explicit Narrative of the Case of Mrs Rudd as Related by Herself* (1775); *Authentic Anecdotes of the Life and Transactions of Mrs Rudd* (1776); *Prudence triumphing over vanity and dissipation or the History of the Life, Character, and Conduct of Mr Robert and Mr Daniel Perreau, and Mrs Rudd* (1776)

Catherine Hayes:
A Narrative of the barbarous and Unheard of Murder of Mr John Hayes (1726); *The Annals of Newgate* by John Villette (1776)

The Sarahs Metyard, mother and daughter:
The Annals of Newgate by John Villette (1776)

Elizabeth Brownrigg:
Genuine and Authentic Account of the Life, Trial and Execution of Elizabeth Brownrigg (1767); *The Trials of James Brownrigg and John Brownrigg* (1767); *The Ordinary of Newgate's Account* by Joseph Moore (1767)

Frances Howard:
A True and Historical Relation of the Poisoning of Thomas Overbury (1651)

Marie-Madeleine d'Aubray:
The Marchioness de Brinvilliers by Gobelin (1676); *The Female Parricide or The History of Mary Margaret d'Aubray, Marchioness de Brinvilliers* (1752)

Poisons:
A Modern Herbal by Mrs M. Grieve (1931); *Poisons and Antidotes* by Carol Turkington (1994)

On page 118: Miss is misquoting a song from *The Maid's Tragedy* by Beaumont and Fletcher (1619):

> Lay a garland on my hearse,
> Of the dismal yew.